THE SURGEON OF LOUGHTON

Ellis Carter

Published by Signo by Artificium

an Artificium Imprint

THE SURGEON OF LOUGHTON
© Ellis Carter 2016

All rights reserved. No part of this publication may be reproduced, stored in a retrieval system, or transmitted in any form or by any means, without the prior permission in writing of the publisher; nor may it be otherwise circulated in any form of binding or cover other than that in which it is published, with these conditions being imposed on any subsequent purchaser.

The right of Ellis Carter to be identified as the author of this work has been asserted in accordance with the Copyright, Designs and Patents Act 1988.

This book is a work of fiction, and except in the case of historical fact, any resemblance to actual persons living or dead is purely coincidental.

A CIP record for this book is available from the British Library.

978-0-9955289-0-1

First Published 2016 by
Signo by Artificium

Printed and bound in Great Britain by
Imprint Digital Ltd

Death:

A punishment to some, to some a gift, and to many a favour.

Seneca

For London's Finest.

CHAPTER ONE

1968

The job was almost done. Six fingers gone, the floor splashed with blood, and the last echo from a scream fading into the stale air of the old warehouse.

Micky the Knife stood up straight and regarded his victim.

The man seated before him had passed out, sagging heavily against the ropes that held him to his chair, his face pointed at the ground. Lengths of spit, snot and blood oozed from his battered nose and mouth and slowly dripped onto the stone floor. His head and left ear were bleeding, the latter split and swollen. Not a pretty sight, not any more. And as for his mutilated fingers...

Micky sniffed in disdain and swapped the snips he was holding into his left hand. 'Wake him up, Clive,' he ordered, glancing sideways at one of his two companions.

A bucketful of ice-cold water was launched at the man in the chair. The shock of it brought him round in an instant. He yelped, snorted, choking for a moment, and his battered head swivelled until his eyes found his torturer again.

'Please,' he rasped. 'No more. *Please*. I'm begging you,'

Micky raised an eyebrow. 'You're begging me?'

'Listen,' spitting out blood with every word, '-you can tell Mr Vincent… tell him, I learnt my lesson. I won't let him down again. I swear,'

Clive, the man holding the now-empty bucket, gave a curt laugh and snorted. 'We ain't telling him *shit*, not on your behalf.' He shifted his weight from foot to foot. 'Do him, Micky,' his voice taking on a keen, excited note. 'You know we ain't got all night,'

The victim began to panic. He rocked violently in the chair, struggling against his restraints.

'No! Wait! Please!'

'Shut your fucking hole! Come on, Mick. Finish it,'

Micky the Knife looked down at his work. He looked at the broken, ruined face and hands of his victim and the sliced fingers lying on the ground at his feet. Wait? Why should he wait? He exhaled evenly and met the eyes of the bleeding man.

'Now, easy does it, Kenneth, pal. You just sit and be quiet. I'm nearly done, see? It'll all be over soon enough.'

He stepped forward. The man in the chair gave another scream, not quite his last, and Micky set to work on finishing the job.

※

Later that evening, Micky paid his employer the necessary visit. Washed and freshly shaven, he'd changed out of his bloodied overalls and into a clean suit. His nearly-new shoes still squeaked when he walked. He took the bus from Trap's Hill through to Leytonstone, and got off three stops early so that he could make the most of the cool night air, taking a certain pleasure at the squeal of the leather as he strode along the pavement.

Inside the club, things would be hot and smoky. At the front entrance Micky edged his way past those waiting hopefully in the queue and gave a nod to the men on the door. They waved him in without a word, and he climbed the red-carpeted stairs knowing that everyone was staring at his back. *That's him, that's The Knife*, he could hear people whispering to one another, and his mouth curled into a sneer.

Music and voices grew louder as he ascended. Another wall of thick, muscular flesh greeted him at the top of the staircase, scrutinising him for a moment before a second door was opened, and then he was inside.

Abruptly the sights, sounds and smells of the Toast Club rushed out, enveloping Micky's slight frame. Men were talking loudly. Women were laughing. A five-piece band played energetically on the stage. Micky walked into a thick fog of cigarette smoke and found himself being suddenly spun about by a pretty blonde in a pink and white dress. She clutched at his shoulders, flashed him her teeth, and puckered her red lips in an airy kiss, before whirling back into the arms of someone else on the dancefloor, shrieking near-hysterically all the while. She smelled of flowers, of whisky and sex.

Micky didn't allow his glance to follow her. He had other things to attend to. Straightening his jacket, brushing down his tie, he headed for the far end of the room where the tables were arranged on three tiers, and as he moved through the haze narrowed his eyes, searching out one face in particular.

Charlie Vincent was already deep in conversation with someone. He had his usual table in the centre at the top, surrounded by his men, his lieutenants. Each one chosen for his sheer physicality; the ability to make a man shrink and shudder with merely a look. God protect you if they actually put a hand on you. Yet Micky was not cowed by their cold eyes, their brutal faces. Even so, he halted at a respectful distance, and with easy patience waited until his employer had finished dealing with his present visitor, watching for the signal that would allow him to approach.

He didn't have to wait for long. The man Charlie was talking to soon started moving aside. The boss lifted a finger and one of his men bent an ear to receive an order or two. No barking instructions, no shouting and screaming: that wasn't Charlie Vincent's style. Micky watched as the lieutenant nodded deferentially at Charlie's commands, and then suddenly there it was; a pointed look his way.

Hauling in a breath, Micky climbed the steps up to the boss' table, and was received with a brisk, business-like smile.

'Good to see you, Michael,'

'And you, Mr Vincent.'

Through the swirling smoke, the large, dark eyes of Charlie Vincent focused upon him. He was sitting casually, leaning on one elbow, a cigarette and a drink in one hand, the other resting on the dark velvet surface of the table. He didn't invite Micky to sit. Instead he stared at him a while whilst the music played and the girls on the dancefloor continued to shriek and laugh. Eventually Charlie took a slow sip from his glass of whisky, then cocked his greying head like a sharp, old vulture perusing something fleshy.

'I'm assuming you've come to bring me some good news?'

Micky's mind flashed back to the warehouse. The blood. The victim, carried out in a rolled-up sheet before being dumped into the canal. 'Yes, Mr Vincent. The problem has been dealt with,'

'Dealt with?' Charlie's lips twitched. 'Permanently?'

'Permanently.' Micky clasped his hands together, fingers entwined, and nodded. 'Just as you asked.'

He restrained a smile of pleasure when he saw the bright gleam in his employer's eyes.

Without shifting his gaze from Micky's face, Charlie Vincent took another sip of whisky. He savoured it, sucking his cheeks in slightly before swallowing. Then he set the glass down on the table and drew himself a long lungful of smoke from his cigarette.

'The Knife strikes again, eh?'

He glanced at one of his men, and without a word the latter reached into a pocket, withdrew a roll of notes, and passed it over to Micky.

Payment. There had never been any doubt that Charlie would settle up. Working for him was easy – if you did exactly what he wanted, when he wanted it. Micky accepted the money with a grateful dip of the head then swiftly pocketed the cash. It wouldn't do to even think about counting it, not in front of the boss.

He looked at Charlie again and was about to ask if he needed him to take care of any other *problems* when, out of the corner of his eye, he noticed someone rapidly approaching the table. Immediately he stiffened; an automatic response to a potential threat.

'Dad!'

Charlie Vincent dropped his cigarette. It fell into the inch of whisky still in his glass and hissed its dying breath just as something small and squealing launched itself into his lap.

The pyjama-clad boy flung his arms around Charlie's neck. No hesitation, no waiting for permission. Charlie's lieutenants and Micky stood watching as their boss wrapped an arm around his son, observing this rare moment as he slipped out of his usual grim, menacing persona into playful father, ticking the boy's arms and gently cuffing his chin.

'Antony, you should be in bed, my lad,'

The boy displayed no fear, no awareness of ceremony, and instead curled up like a cat onto his father's knees. 'Auntie May let me stay up 'cos it's Saturday tomorrow,' he said. He glanced around at those watching and his eyes – large and dark like Charlie's – alighted on Micky. They stared at one another until the kid grew tired of the game and said, 'Can I sit up with you for a bit, Dad? I'm not tired,'

Charlie's grunt of disapproval faded into the background. Again at the edge of Micky's vision, a woman, dressed casually yet effectively in a pale sweater and straight skirt, came towards them. She had a quick, purposeful walk, and seemed to ignore the looks of the other patrons as she brushed past their tables. Without missing a beat she strode up to Charlie Vincent and scooped the child from his father's embrace.

'Aha! So this is where you got to. Now look Tony,' she chided the boy, 'I didn't say you could come in here,'

Micky watched as the boss allowed himself to be parted from his son. He watched as Mr Vincent ruffled the six year old's head of inky black curls before lighting another cigarette, and waited for the inevitable change of expression.

It didn't disappoint. Charlie shot his sister a dark look. 'Take him back upstairs to bed. Now,'

'Sorry. He gets easily excited. Won't sleep. You know what he's like,'

'I know what you're like.'

The cold exchange made Micky uneasy. May Vincent, Charlie's little sister, was the apple of every man's eye in East London. There was none of her brother's thin-lipped brutality about her. She was soft, voluptuous, clever too: the only girl Micky knew who could have a conversation about more than hairstyles and mini-skirts. But she was off-limits to most admirers, and even for the few who Charlie would have considered worthy of his sister, there was still danger. No man could dare risk putting a foot wrong if he courted May. Charlie had had men beaten half to death just for wearing the wrong colour tie to a business meeting in the club. Imagine the horrors that might await a suitor or a fiancé who forgot May's birthday, or who turned up late for a date? For most men, it simply didn't bear thinking about.

Micky the Knife however was not most men. He looked at May and thought about her smile, and felt a warmth begin to spread through his chest.

Charlie's brusqueness with his sister did not appear to phase her. She alone could risk ignoring his sour looks. Instead she swung the six year old up onto her hip. 'Say goodnight to Daddy,'

Now the boss was smiling again: 'I'll see you in the morning, Tony.' When the boy gave a disappointed frown he added, 'We'll see about getting you sorted with that new bike you wanted, eh?'

Tony's little face lit up. He didn't protest as his aunt turned, heading back the way she had come, towards a side door and the stairs beyond that led to the flat above. As she moved, Micky watched her. It was impossible not to, even standing so close to Charlie, so close to danger. He had long held a candle for May, and the hint of her perfume that he caught as she walked off made the flesh on his throat tingle with excitement. But she hadn't even glanced in his direction. She was wise like that. His heart shuddered momentarily and he tightened his lips to keep himself from sighing in disappointment.

Realising that the interruption was over and that Charlie was scrutinising him again, Micky glanced at his boss uneasily. Raising his voice above the music, he said: 'Is there anything else you'd like me to do for you, Mr Vincent?'

The two men eyed one another. Charlie looked to be thinking, turning something over and over in his mind. Finally he took a long, slow drag on his cigarette and blew a stream of smoke across the table towards him.

'Not right now, Michael, thank you.' He pointed at the bar. 'Before you leave, go get yourself a drink. On me,'

'Cheers, Mr Vincent. I will,'

'I'll be in touch again when I've something useful for you to do.'

He didn't wait to risk being told to piss off more brusquely than that. Micky nodded his thanks and was soon weaving his way through the crowd again, breathing more easily with every step. This time he avoided all drunken blondes. At the bar he caught the eye of one of the waiters and was rewarded with a whiskey sour. It vanished in one gulp.

The waiter, watching this, lifted his eyebrow and silently asked: did he want another?

Micky shook his head. One drink in this place was more than enough. He straightened his shirt cuffs, and as he did so noticed how slippery his hands had become.

He flexed his damp fingers, thought of May again.

'Fucking Christ. You must be mental.'

It was time to leave.

CHAPTER TWO

2016

There were rats in the garden again. He'd laid out traps, baited with fat-enrobed poison, and had caught two. Neither were very large unfortunately, and weren't worth keeping. Micky inspected their stiffened corpses. Males. He sighed and tossed them into the bin. The pregnant girls were so hard to catch. He put the traps back along the bottom edge of the fence, and hoped for better luck next time.

Rats were a problem for Micky. Over the years he'd shared his home with them occasionally, and almost got used to them eating his bed, his carpets, and his food. Sometimes they chewed through electrical cables and died, stinking the place out for a while. Yet all that was easy to ignore, at least in comparison to the damage they'd do if they ever got into his workshop again.

Ah, the workshop. Sited at the foot of the garden. There, he kept his collection. His best, most favoured and most fragile possessions. If the rats found a way inside they could wreak havoc, and had on two previous occasions.

1988: he'd left the door open for a while during the hot summer, and some of the little bastards had broken the perimeter. They'd chewed at a Muntjac, two badgers and a scene with a family group of hares that it tore his heart to have to discard, it was so badly damaged. And then of course there was '94, when Pikey thieves smashed into the place and took his power tools. Thanks to those shitbags, the rats got in again and this time targeted his bird collection. He'd gone into the workshop one morning to find the floor littered with feathers and ruined hawks, crows, owls and the remains of his prize Osprey mounting. Bugger the power tools; that Osprey had been a loss difficult to accept.

When he'd gotten over the shock and anger, Micky had come to a conclusion: that the old wooden workshop where he practised his taxidermist's art would have to be rebuilt. So, in the autumn of that year he'd emptied his savings account, packed up his equipment, and put his remaining collection into storage temporarily whilst workmen demolished the old building and erected a new, steel-framed, aluminium- and zinc-clad one instead.

It had taken him a couple of days' hard graft to move all the birds and animals into the storage place, ferrying them about in his old Mercedes 280SEL. The receptionist had watched with wary curiosity as the old man came and went, unloading his dogs, deer, rabbits and other creatures, all fixed forever in their frozen poses. Micky had felt the heat of the woman's gaze, sensed the distaste flowing out from her, but it hadn't bothered him. He knew what most people thought. Taking the carcasses of dead birds and animals, stripping out the meat, preparing and curing the skin, stretching it over wire frames, packing and sewing it all back up so that it took on a lifelike form again: these things were not for the squeamish. 'It's so horribly *ghoulish,*' one of his neighbours had said to him, back in a time when he'd been more open with others about his art. The man had looked around the workshop with evident horror. 'I don't know how you can stand to do it. All those rotting guts to deal with. And then being surrounded by dozens of pairs of glass eyes all the time. It would give me the bloody creeps.' Micky hadn't told the twee little prick that he'd done worse, much worse, in years gone by. And to men, not animals. No, he'd said nothing of that. Instead he'd vowed that no one living would be invited into his workshop ever again if he could help it, and so far he'd stuck to that promise.

Dead rats disposed of, Micky shuffled back down the garden. The hinges on the workshop door squealed softly as he opened it, and he stepped over the raised threshold as quickly as his seventy-one year old hips would allow. He then locked himself inside and snapped on the light.

Four fluorescent strips illuminated the room. In a space six metres by eight, wildlife climbed the walls in a display so vivid, so real, he could almost imagine he could hear the twitter of starlings, the sniff and grunt of foraging badgers, and the anxious thud of deer hooves running for cover. Dogs stood to attention or laid couchant, looking out with bright eyes and varnished noses. A pair of hares reared up on hind legs to box, whilst a milky-white barn owl soared with outstretched wings above. Cats prowled the shelves, and just beneath the roof a small flock of gulls and skuas filled his little aluminium sky.

'Morning, boys and girls. Beautiful day for it.'

Micky's face broke with a wrinkled smile. This scene was his, of his design and creation, and it never failed to please him. He stood and marvelled at all this for a while, and then he set to work.

In one corner of the workshop there was a large chest freezer where he stored the new stock. He shuffled towards it and lifted the heavy lid. A white, frozen fog oozed out over the lip. Without hesitation, Micky plunged his hands into its depths. He knew what he was feeling for. Fingers closed around the stiffened body of the lamb and he hauled it up from its icy grave. A barren, half-closed eye met his.

'Think it's time you were defrosted, son,' he told it, and shut the freezer door.

※

The workshop was quiet, just as he liked it. Peaceful, serene, though the air was thick with the smell of chemicals and old fur. In the centre of the room Micky was busy with his current project. Seated at his long work bench, he pored over the delicate operation of skinning a small fox. Face bent close to the dead vixen, he carefully separated flesh from pelt with the sensitive, precise touch of an expert. The fox had apparently been poisoned and had thus died intact. Road-killed animals, with their crushed skulls and violently burst abdomens, presented more of a challenge and often required patching to look their best – if they were worth bothering with at all. But this vixen was delightfully pristine, lacking only her blood and her breath. When he finally extracted the last leg and the skull from the fur, Micky sat back, cocked his head, and smiled at his work. She was going to make a wonderful display.

He reached for a cup of milky tea now cooling at his elbow. Around him, in a precise formation, the tools of his trade were arranged. Knives, scalpels, a hack saw, wire cutters and several sets of pliers, amongst other implements, all waited to be utilised. As he downed several mouthfuls of the tea, he thought about the next step – preserving the hide – and pictured the fox finished and mounted, its orange-hued fur bright and gleaming, glass eyes reflecting the light. The prospect made the old man's heart beat a little faster.

He glanced towards the lamb he'd fetched from the freezer. The little, twisted carcass hung from a hook protruding from a shelf. It was slowly defrosting, and would be ready for skinning by morning. He planned to use it in a scene with the fox. The contrast of predator and prey was one he had returned to many times, and it never failed to satisfy him. Minutes ticked by as Micky visualised his completed project, looking at it from all angles in his head. This imagining of the end product was almost as enjoyable as the actual creation of it, or so he found.

It was only the distant blaring of a car horn that finally broke his reverie.

The day was wearing on. With a grunt and a sigh, Micky prised himself up from his seat. He wrapped the unwanted parts of the vixen in newspaper and looked around at his work again. Amidst the completed wildlife adorning the ceiling and walls, and the larger pieces arranged around the perimeter of the floor, Micky felt most at home. This was his special place. His place of thought, of work, of solitude. Of course he kept it all scrupulously clean. Each animal was routinely inspected, brushed, dusted and admired. The work surface was immaculate, and he swept and disinfected the floor every other day. Insects were vacuumed up, and though he didn't chase away any spiders that he found, they were actively discouraged from stringing their webs between the exhibits. The workshop was a museum to his craft, and Micky was fiercely determined that it should always be immaculate.

At the other end of the garden though, the house was quite a different story. With hunger growling in his belly, Micky took the fox's wrapped innards, locking the workshop securely behind him, and shuffled up the overgrown garden path towards his home. The neighbours on both sides had allowed their conifers to grow thick and tall, giving his garden privacy but robbing him of the best of the sunlight. Not that he minded. Any faint ideas he might once have had about growing flowers and vegetables in his garden had long since vanished. Now that the commuters had moved into that part of Loughton, the street was mostly quiet during the day, and no one bothered the old man in his post-war bungalow with its rotten windows, overgrown shrubbery, and ancient Mercedes parked on the driveway. In the main, Micky was content to be ignored. He'd long since lost patience with and interest in most of the rest of the world. For him, his taxidermy hobby was now the centre of his universe.

'I'm happy enough,' he told himself, not entirely convincingly, and with a frown dropped the little wrapped package into the wheelie bin. He saw it land on top of the dead rats in the instant before he slammed the lid shut.

The keys to the workshop jangled in his hand. Micky looked down at them and remembered; remembered sitting on the bus from the prison, years ago, looking haggard and feeling bewildered. All he'd had to his name then had been the contents of a small duffle bag and the four quid the prison authorities had bunged him to get out of Yorkshire. But inside the duffle bag, pinned to the lining, he'd found an envelope. And in it, a set of house keys. A tag attached had given him the address, and a scribbled note confirmed the benefactor:

You earned this Michael – C.V.

Micky shivered at the memory. 'Yeah. I earned it alright.'

Old times. Funny how, of late, the recollections seemed to come to him more frequently. He put the workshop keys in his trouser pocket and allowed himself a second or two more to visualise getting off that bus and walking down the street, scanning each house until he found the bungalow, of which he was now the new owner. He saw himself standing in front of the unfamiliar door and remembered not knowing whether to laugh, cry, or run screaming into the distance.

Seventy-one year old Micky tilted his head and looked up at the house. Back then the paint had all been fresh, the gardens neat, and there'd been no rat infestation. But some things hadn't changed in forty-odd years. He was still alone.

The door to the kitchen was unlocked and he shuffled inside. Here, there was a different aroma. No preserving chemicals, disinfectant or smell of old blood. Instead the kitchen was rank with the sour stink of unwashed dishes. Plates and bowls were piled up in the sink in a few inches of rancid, grey water. Mould grew on the window ledge and dirt and grease lined the floor and work surfaces. The cooker was no longer white, now encased in a thick, dark gunge studded with the odd dried bean, piece of pasta or pea, and layered with spatterings of sauce. Old newspapers and junk mail were stacked high on the little kitchen table, leaving no space to sit and eat.

Micky opened a cupboard and pondered the selection of tins. He ate simply and sparingly, mostly processed foods. On a Friday night he fetched himself bread, a pound of bacon and six eggs, and enjoyed fried breakfasts on Saturdays and Sundays. Since there was no room at the table, he ate most of his meals standing up, balancing his plate on his hand and cutting his food with the side of his fork as he stared out of the kitchen window down towards the workshop, always thinking, always pondering his next creation.

From the cupboard he finally selected a tin of beans and heated them in a grubby, unwashed pan, demolishing them quickly as he thought about the lamb and the fox. After cramming the pan and his spoon into the sink, Micky wandered through to his living room. There, things were no better. He lived predominantly in that single space, on a narrow bed pushed into one corner, separated from his sofa and the television by a pile of unwashed laundry. The latter gave off a mouldy odour when disturbed, and Micky edged past it carefully. His bones creaked as he sank down onto the sofa. With a grunt he reached for the television remote and flicked the screen into life.

The large flatscreen was his only nod to modernity in the old house. The walls still bore the paint and paper they were decorated with fifty years before, and the carpets, never changed, were threadbare in places, otherwise grey with dust. Micky's bungalow had never felt a woman's touch in all the time he'd lived there. Long ago he'd held hopes that things would be different, but those dreams were soon dashed, and ever since he'd lived the life of a resigned bachelor.

Another memory taunted him. He glanced up warily. This one would hurt, he knew.

On a shelf beyond the colourful display of the television, a rectangular frame held a scene of faces, black and white and faded now. It was Christmas '68 at the Toast Club, and Charlie Vincent sat in the centre of the picture with his arms around two pneumatic blondes. A youthful Micky was grinning a lopsided grin somewhere over Charlie's right shoulder, amidst a host of other gangland characters, all long gone. Yet one particular face stood out amongst the others. He squinted to bring her image into focus, and saw again that too familiar, perfect pale skin and jet black hair. The only woman he'd ever loved.

He couldn't have her. A miserable truth. And, after years of lonely desperation, fresh from prison, he'd tried to fill the void she'd left in him by buying himself a dog, a Jack Russell. Bert. The dog had lived nine years with Micky in the bungalow, bringing him some small comfort until it ran out one morning to join in with some kids playing on the street and never came back. With this fresh hole torn through his heart he'd sworn never to let himself be hurt again. It was easier, Micky found, to console himself by ignoring the living and focusing on bringing the dead shells of animals back to life instead.

In time he stopped thinking about lost Bert. But she, the woman, was much harder to forget.

Knowing that painful feelings of loss and loneliness were about to swamp him, Micky changed channels on the television, searching for something that would divert his attention, lighten the mood. He found an episode of *Kojak* and settled on that. It should have kept the past at bay, but halfway through the programme a female suspect with dark hair, a sensuous mouth and eyes that flashed at the detective's forthright accusations, made him think and again he found himself glancing towards the photo on the shelf.

Just an image now, an insubstantial copy of the real Her. Micky stared miserably at the tiny image of May Vincent, taken at her brother's club all those years ago, and when he felt his aged eyes begin to sting he shut them tight, praying that one day, somehow, he would finally forget.

The Surgeon of Loughton

CHAPTER THREE

2016

The office above Bar 101 nightclub was as busy during the day as it was at night. At all hours from the early morning it seemed that people were coming and going. Men came up from the club, bringing piles of cash for the boss, not all of which came from the tills. Others came in off the street, their clothes smelling of the cold air and their pockets full of mobile phones, stuff in small bags, and more cash. Why anyone would need more than one phone, Micky couldn't fathom, but it seemed the norm these days. He watched the visitors hammer out messages with their thumbs and squawk loudly when they took a call. He thought about the early days, when people didn't understand the technology and thought they had to shout down the bloody receiver when someone called from the other side of town. Wryly, he smiled to himself, thinking some things hadn't changed.

Micky observed everyone who came to speak with his boss, Tony Vincent. There were plenty these days with foreign accents: Eastern Europeans, West Africans, the occasional Turk. Sometimes they smiled, greeting his boss with handshakes, nods, or – if they dared, and if he allowed it – a wide-armed embrace, perhaps a friendly slap to the back. Mostly they were more reticent, nervous even, scanning the room, eyeing everyone and everything. A few wanted to talk in private and sometimes Tony would oblige, his expression dark and serious. Other times he'd growl and tell them to *sit the fuck down*. They always did as they were told, even though Micky could tell from their sour faces that one or two of them weren't used to taking orders.

Micky worked three days a week for Tony, supplementing his state pension with a few light duties: make the tea, keep the place tidy, get Tony his lunch. It wasn't like it was in the old days when he worked for Charlie Vincent. Back then it was, *cut that fucker's throat, Micky;* or, *make sure so-and-so never walks again*. But those times were long gone. The Toast Club was long gone. Yet Tony's place – Bar 101 – was much the same in many respects. The three-storey building held a nightclub, a couple of private function rooms, Tony's personal office suite, and on the top floor an apartment. Tony only used the latter if business was brisk and he didn't want to drive back to Chigwell at night, or if he had one of the girls he kept 'on the side' in to entertain him. Like his father, Tony had an eye for blondes. And, also like his old man, he ran a drug trafficking ring, handled vast quantities of illicit and stolen goods, and had no time for men who couldn't follow orders. Just like the old basement at the Toast, where Charlie's men took you if you were acting up in the club, the courtyard out the back of Bar 101 had seen plenty of blood and smashed limbs and faces. Tony had learned from his father: don't be afraid of using violence to protect your end.

Charlie Vincent had been a difficult boss to work for. He'd been hard to get to know, easy to offend, and quick to jump straight to an order of torture or worse if a situation frustrated him. Tony was more easy-going. You could have a laugh with him, tell him a joke and not worry that he might have you beaten up if he didn't find it funny. That said, he wasn't exactly even-tempered. He could often explode with anger, and was much more vocal than his old man. And as for reputation... Charlie would have been proud. It was said that Tony had killed three people, all ex-business associates, and was so slippery that the Old Bill had given up ever trying to prosecute him for the murders. If it was true, and there was little doubt in Micky's mind that it was, then it was better to be on Tony's good side and avoid becoming victim number four.

Still, despite the risks, it was useful to have the job being Tony's part-time office helper. In his youth Micky had failed to see the point of savings, and if it hadn't been for Charlie Vincent gifting him the bungalow he'd have been living in a Council flat all these years. The money Tony gave him as wages ensured he could buy the supplies he needed for his taxidermy. He stayed away from getting involved in any of Tony's work, however. All that belonged in the past. '82 had been the last time Micky had had to wipe a man's blood from his hands, and since then he'd used his tools and talents strictly on feather and fur. He was no longer Micky the Knife. Now he was just Old Micky, arthritic, and usually smelling of stale, unwashed clothes.

Few who came to Tony's place knew anything about the old fella with the thin, grey hair, lopsided mouth and hunched gait. If they paid him any attention it was to laugh at his scruffiness, or sniff in disgust at how he smelled. That day was no different. A succession of young men came and went, and Micky offered them all tea and hospitality whilst they waited for Tony. But one in particular, a six foot African with a cleft lip and a black, dangerous glare, took things too far.

When the man entered the office, Micky shuffled over to this latest visitor with a mug of hot tea. 'Tony's just downstairs. He'll be back in a tick. Here you go, son, make yourself comfortable.'

He proffered the drink, not expecting the African to lash out. One large fist smashed the mug out of the old man's hands and his face contorted.

'Get the fuck away from me, you stupid bastard!'

The mug flew to the floor, shattering into pieces. It sprayed the nearby furniture and Micky's trousers with hot tea. His old eyes looked up into the African's face and silence fell across the room.

A few of Tony's men who were sitting on the nearby sofas stiffened at this sign of trouble. Micky sensed hands reaching into pockets, knives being flicked open. It was all about to kick off. He heard his own heartbeat quickening and beyond it the snorted breaths of the African, now towering over him.

'Easy fella,' he tried to calm the situation. 'It's just a tea,'

'I don't want your *piss*,' the man snarled. 'I didn't come here for that. I came to speak to the boss,'

It was difficult to be sure, his eyes were so dark, but the visitor's pupils looked dilated, suggesting he was under the influence of something. Micky lowered his gaze and looked down at the spilled tea. Even if he'd been forty or fifty years younger, there was no sense arguing and getting into a fight with someone high on drugs. Not when you weren't carrying a weapon.

A voice suddenly sliced through the air. 'What the fuck is this?'

Tony was standing in the doorway, mobile phone held loosely at his ear. Entering the office he'd stopped, scanned the scene, and was now glaring at the African. His jaw ground. His eyes slid to the mess on the floor and then he looked at Micky.

'Clean that shit up, Micky mate,' he said in a tight voice, and then as the old man nodded and scuttled off, Tony shut the door behind him and advanced into the room.

'You came to my place just to fuck up the décor, did you Solly?' he said to the African. 'Is this how you do things in fucking Lagos? Is it? Eh?'

'No Tony. I came because there is a problem,'

'A problem? With what?' Now circling his visitor.

'With those girls you sent me. Two have run away and the other refuses to work. I need replacements,'

'Well that sounds like your problem, Solly.' Tony stopped moving. The phone was still in his hand but he had lowered it to his side. 'And you didn't answer my question.' He pointed down at the broken cup. 'I said, what the fuck is THIS?'

Micky, his back turned and rummaging through a cupboard in the little kitchenette, hunting for a dishcloth, didn't see what happened next. He only heard it. There was a dull thud and then a yelp and a groan, and something heavy fell to the floor. When he looked around he saw the African sprawled amidst broken chunks of porcelain, bent double and clutching his stomach. His face was contorted with pain, and when he dared to lift his head Tony drew back one foot and kicked him hard in the face.

The man crumpled again.

When it was over, which was not for another half minute or so, Tony stepped back and glared around the room. His cheeks and brow looked flushed.

'No one—,' he barked, '—comes into my club and starts fucking about like this. No one! And no one lays a finger on Micky. You all got that? Yeah?'

The man on the floor was coughing up blood and at least a couple of his teeth. Tony snarled contemptuously at him.

'Anything this piece of shit wants, tell him he can fucking *forget* it. He can come back and see me when he's learned some fucking *manners*.'

Furiously, the boss stalked over to the other end of the office and threw himself into his chair. He smoothed his thick, dark hair with a hand. Everyone watched as Tony put the phone back to his ear and, as though nothing had happened, resumed his call, suddenly cool as could be.

When Solly had dragged himself up from the floor and fucked off, the mood in the office cautiously began to return to normal. Only Micky, avoiding the glances of the others, continued to feel on edge. He cleaned up the mess, including the blood and the dentistry, and spent the rest of the afternoon in a mood. He felt slighted, diminished by how the black man had spoken to him, and even worse when he thought how he'd had to rely on Tony to come to his aid. *If the old gang could see me now,* he thought, and shuddered.

Eventually it was time to head home. Micky was glad to be able to pull on his well-worn overcoat and shuffle downstairs, eager to put the events of the day behind him. In the car park at the back of the club, the familiar smell of his old Mercedes welcomed him as he climbed inside, much less lithely than when he'd bought it back in '68. The car had long been a prized possession, but the old girl was routinely disappointing him now. He put the key in the ignition and grimaced, expecting her to stutter and fail, but was relieved when the engine groaned awkwardly into life.

'Jesus. Makes a bloody change.'

Micky fastened his seatbelt and slid his hands around the wheel. She'd covered more than 268,000 miles, and there wasn't a lot left in her forty-eight year old body. The two-tone silver and black paintwork was scratched, chipped and fading. The engine needed maintenance at annoyingly frequent intervals, and seemed to grow thirstier with every tank of fuel it guzzled. Most of the electrics had failed at one time or another. None of the heaters worked any more, and even the radio could be temperamental. As he slowly backed out of the car park Micky glanced around at the other motors. Next to Tony's gleaming black Range Rover there were two enormous BMWs, along with a Jaguar and a Lexus, and a selection of sportier coupés. In comparison his old barge-like Merc looked worn out, an arthritic hangover from a distant past. Resentfully he gritted his teeth and shifted the old girl into gear. 'Looks like I'm stuck with you, and you with me,' he muttered as she pulled lethargically out onto the main road.

He drove out through east London, into the suburbs and towards home. He was still smarting from the day's humiliation. 'That stupid jig made me look a right fool,' he growled. 'Small and weak. Me! It wouldn't have been like that forty-odd years ago.' Back then, no one would have slapped a drink out of Micky the Knife's hands, not unless they wanted to be found in a shallow grave with their throat cut or their guts hacked out. His age-spotted hands gripped the steering wheel a little tighter. Tony had had to help him out, and to everyone watching it said that Micky couldn't handle things himself. He had to rely on someone else to do his fighting for him now. He glowered at his own reflection in the rear view mirror. 'If me old mates saw that, I'd be a bleedin' laughing stock.'

But they were gone. All gone. Charlie Vincent had dropped dead from a heart attack in the early eighties. Turf wars, prison, old age and various accidents, genuine or arranged, had steadily worn away the rest of the gang, leaving Micky the last man standing. And as for May...

He sniffed, sighed. 'Funny how things work out, ain't it?'

In his mind's eye he was suddenly back in the Toast Club. Pushing through the door from the main room out into the stairwell, leaving the music and the laughter behind for a minute. A headache, if he remembered rightly. Been up two days straight waiting for someone who'd gotten into Charlie's bad books to come home. But the prey had evaded him; probably had a tip off that Micky the Knife had been told to do him in. In the stairwell Micky stopped, faltered when he saw her sat on the steps and smoking a cigarette, a cup of tea in one hand and her feet in slippers. But still beautiful, just as she always was.

'Alright, May.' Micky licked his lips, tried to come up with something else to say. 'Can't get you anything stronger, can I?'

She lifted her eyebrows. 'I don't think my big brother would appreciate you plying me with gin, Micky,'

'Guess he wouldn't.' He put his hands into the pockets of his suit jacket. 'Mind if I have one of those?'

'Be my guest.'

She offered him the packet of cigarettes and he took one, relieved that his hand didn't tremble when he caught her smiling at him. In the few seconds it took to light the thing and take his first drag his brain worked furiously, desperate to think of the right words to say.

'So. Charlie's got you on babysitting duty again, has he?'

She shrugged. It was an idle gesture but one that thinly concealed resentment. 'That's my life these days. Just a glorified servant. Still,' cigarette now at her lips, 'aren't we all?'

Micky looked uncomfortable momentarily. She'd struck a nerve. He tried to change the subject.

'It must have been hard for Charlie, losing his old lady so sudden. We all felt for him, and for the boy,'

'Hard for Charlie?' May stared. Suddenly she laughed, a sharp sound, devoid of humour. 'He probably doesn't even remember what Teresa looked like,'

'That's a bit harsh,'

'Is it?' her voice was cold. 'Talks about her, does he? The woman he was married to for eight years. The mother of his child. Brings her up in conversation? Tries to keep her memory alive, that right?'

Micky frowned and peered closely at his cigarette. The hard, intense look on May's face was making him uneasy. 'Well, not exactly—,'

She exhaled, watching him. 'No, I didn't think so.' A clump of ash spilled onto her knee and she flicked it away. Slowly her face and her tone softened again. 'Charlie has it easy. He can switch off his feelings. I wish I could.' Another drag of her cigarette. 'I wish I could forget seeing Teresa like a bloody skeleton, watching the cancer eat her alive.' With a shudder and a shake of her head, she exhaled the grey smoke and rubbed at her cheek. 'Still, at least Tony doesn't remember any of that. Poor little sod.'

They fell quiet, just the raucous sounds of the club in the background and the pulse of Micky's heart beating loudly in his mouth. This encounter wasn't working out the way he wanted it to. He wanted to make May laugh, make her smile. He'd never been absolutely sure if she liked him but she'd certainly never told him to piss off. And there had been that Christmas Eve party when she'd chuckled at one of his jokes. Maybe there was hope?

'Anyway,' she broke the silence for him. 'What you doing out here with me? Shouldn't you be in there, dancing with one of those girls?'

He grinned awkwardly. 'Never been much of a dancer,'

'No?'

'No,'

She smiled. At last. 'Pity,' looking him straight in the eye.

Micky felt his heart quicken. 'You like to dance, then?'

'Well, I used to. Sometimes, not very often mind, I'd meet someone wasn't so afraid of my brother that he couldn't ask me out on the dancefloor.' Her eyes seemed to sparkle, and she looked him up and down before returning to hold his gaze.

This was it, he knew. This was the moment. He blew the last of the smoke out of his lungs and clenched his lips together, preparing the words. May watched him expectantly. Any second, any second now he would...

A sudden jolt, a woman's squeal, and the din from the club exploded into the stairwell. A man and a woman, both drunk, had staggered through the door. The man's hand was already undoing the buttons on the front of the woman's dress. But he realised he'd bumped into something, into someone, and he turned and blearily caught sight of Micky.

'Sorry pal, didn't mean to—,'

He blinked once, twice, then recognition hit him. The laugh died quickly on the intruder's lips and he backed off, throwing up a hand in apology.

Micky was already bristling.

'Pal? I'm your *pal*, am I?'

'Jesus Christ! Sorry. I didn't realise. I—,'

The intruder was floundering now. Face suddenly as white as bone, the man grabbed hold of his girl's arm and didn't care if she yelped in pain as he dragged her back into the club. Micky glared after them through the porthole window in the door. A mixture of emotions surged through him: anger, resentment, triumph. When they settled and he grew calm again he turned back to May – but saw at once that the moment, his moment, was lost.

She was stubbing out her cigarette on the stone step. May dropped the smouldering dog-end into the remains of her tea. 'I'd better get back up to the flat, check on Tony,' she told him, the sparkle gone from her gaze.

He nodded, deflated. 'Right. Yeah. Well, I'll let you get on,'

She got to her feet. Smoothed down her skirt, then when that was done hesitated for a second. 'See you around, Michael,' she said. 'Michael the Knife,'

There was a hint of something in her voice. Not quite a smile, but still. Micky looked at her with what he hoped was his most soulful glance.

She didn't react to it. Instead only turned and padded up the staircase, slippers slapping against her stockinged feet, leaving him in a state of confusion, irritated at himself. When he heard the door to the flat shut firmly, he shook himself, scrubbed a hand through his hair and hissed a curse.

'Fucking twat! Bloody idiot!'

So near, and yet so far.

Brooding now, dreaming of the old times, of the old him, Old Micky drove as fast as the Merc would allow, which was not much of a speed at all. He left the city behind, taking a longer route along the A121 that scythed through the forest. It was tea-time, somewhere in the too-short lull between the school run madness and the scramble home by the city's commuters, and he reckoned he had just enough time to see if there was anything of use lying by the side of the tarmac.

Road kill provided a supply of animals for Micky's taxidermy. Most days he could spot something, although only a few ever turned out to be suitable. The big, heavy vehicles squashed most of the subjects, damaging them well beyond repair. What he really needed was something that had been bumped, thrown clear of the carriageway and onto the verge, perhaps with its neck broken but otherwise intact. Today he was in luck. A carcass, fat and freshly mown down, suddenly caught his eye and he swiftly indicated, swinging the intractable Mercedes over to the side.

Abruptly his mood changed. Gone was the heavy cloud of gloom invoked by the day's events and old memories: now he was reinvigorated. Micky hopped out from the car. He could be relatively quick and light on his feet when he needed to be, and feeling a thrill of excitement he hurried back a few metres up the road, ignoring the traffic and the curious looks from other drivers, to investigate what lay there.

The badger was slumped on its side, paws together and motionless, as though merely sleeping. Micky reached out and laid a hand on its belly. Still warm. Good. There was no obvious damage to the creature; clearly a car had side-swiped it and it had died from the shock and internal bleeding. He nodded to himself and stroked the beast, feeling its firm skull beneath the striped fur.

'I'll take care of you now, son,' he murmured to it.

As the traffic sped by Micky collected the dead animal and carried it back to his car with all the gentle care of a parent cradling its fallen child. When the badger was secured, he climbed back inside the Mercedes, and with a much lighter heart than before, headed straight home.

CHAPTER FOUR

2016

He cut the sandwiches with a carving knife. It was the sharpest one available in the kitchenette, but even so it could only just manage to saw messily through two slices of white bread and thin layers of ham, cheese and butter.

Still, Micky persevered, even though his hands were beginning to hurt. A couple of hours earlier he'd been dunking animal hides into buckets of preserving chemicals and now his skin felt tight. He grimaced and plated up yet another round of sandwiches. Youngsters had been coming and going all day, and they all seemed to be hungry and needed feeding. Round after round of tea and grub left the kitchen, and Micky barely had time to make anything for himself. He eyed the young lads disapprovingly: most of them were far too cocky, overconfident in their abilities, and that usually led to fuck ups. They were flash, brash, and wouldn't have survived ten minutes back in the sixties, he told himself. Grudgingly, he served them their snacks and imagined them pissing themselves in terror as Micky the Knife prepared to slice off their lips and eyelids.

It was Friday afternoon and something was up. Tony seemed to be in a pensive mood. He let one of his lieutenants – a squat, broad-shouldered Northerner called George – deal with all the comings and goings, and instead sat in his chair at the far end of the room, frowning at his phone and ignoring everyone.

The day wore on, but Tony's temper didn't improve. Just before four, as Micky was elbow-deep in washing-up and the office was quiet, he heard a mass of boots hurrying up the back staircase. Alarm made him tense up momentarily: a police raid. He shot the boss an anxious look, but Tony appeared stoic. He'd turned about in his chair and was looking at the door. A moment later a group of five young men burst into the room, and the boss got up and walked towards them.

They were breathing hard, faces flushed. From the kitchenette Micky watched as Tony's dark gaze flicked from one man to the next. The boss put his hands to his hips, revealing the edge of his gold Patek Philippe beneath the cuff of his blue shirt. 'Well?' he demanded, and he tightened his mouth. 'Make me happy. Give me the news,'

The men looked at one another, and at the floor. *This ain't good*, Micky thought to himself. He soaped a plate and placed it gently on the draining board, so as not to disturb the scene.

'Come on! Somebody!' Tony boomed, and his face turned black. 'I ain't got all pissing day!'

At last, one of the group spoke up. 'The rumour's true, Boss,' the man said nervously, eyes shifty and haunted, 'They've found him. They've found the Turk's body.'

This news brought silence to the room. Suddenly the only thing anyone could hear was Micky cautiously rattling the dishes around in the sink. Realising this, the old man glanced around and caught Northern George giving him a dirty look.

'I knew it!' Tony snarled. 'I knew you cunts would let me down. How many times did I say it? Make sure you get rid of him properly! Now all the Filth in East London's going to be on my back, sniffing around my business.' He ran a hand through his hair and started pacing back and forth. 'Someone's going to pay for this.' He paused, jabbed a finger at the crew. 'And I'll make one thing clear: it *ain't* going to be *me*.'

The atmosphere in the office was tense. Micky waited, watching discreetly from the corner of his eye. He picked up a tea towel and began drying a cup, conscious that at any second the situation could explode. Tony was now ranting and raving at his men, reminding them that the late Burak Dal – a nasty-looking Turk recently arrived from Germany, who was trying to muscle in on Tony's drug business – was potentially about to do more damage dead than he ever had when alive.

'What did I say?' Tony was poking one of his guys hard in the chest. 'You don't shit where you eat! You should've taken his body down to the coast, not buried him in a shallow fucking grave in my backyard!'

At that point, one of the group decided he should try and defend their actions. 'Boss, we did our best—,'

'Yeah, we thought the Old Bill was onto us,' said another, eager to try and pacify things.

It was a terrible mistake.

'Your best?' Tony stared at the men incredulously. 'Are you taking the piss?' He spun about and looked at Northern George. 'Are you hearing this? Am *I* fucking hearing this?'

'I should have handled it, Boss,' George told him, and his eyes narrowed as he looked at the hapless gang. 'This lot are all morons,'

By now Tony Vincent's face had turned a violent shade of purple. Micky shrank back against the kitchen sink. He recalled the old days, when Charlie had cause to discipline any of his gang. The results had always been bloody – and quite often fatal. When Tony motioned towards George and said, 'Listen, give me your shooter,' Micky saw in him the reflection of his old man, and he prepared himself to witness another murder.

Northern George reached into the pocket of his jacket. When the men saw the pistol emerge, wrapped loosely in chamois, they all started protesting their innocence, all blaming one another, or the Old Bill for being too smart on this one. But Tony wasn't listening. He took the gun from George, checked it over, and saw that it was loaded. He then wiped it down, lifted it using a corner of the chamois, and shoved it onto the hands of the man nearest.

'One last choice,' he said. 'Take this, go outside, and find a field somewhere. Not around here, you mugs! Then decide between you who wants to live and take their chances with me, and who just wants to blow their own head off and get it over with.'

He scanned all five jabbering idiots.

'None of you pricks are any use to me. If you don't want me bashing your heads in, which believe me I am more than happy to do, right now, then you can take care of it yourselves.' Tony shrugged, as though unconcerned about the choice they might make, though his eyes revealed the truth. 'It's up to you. Now, GET THE FUCK OUT OF MY CLUB!'

At this signal, Northern George started swinging his fists, landing punches and kicking the group, and the men bolted as one. They fought with each other to be the first out of the door. They fled down the stairs, George giving chase, screaming and cursing at them as they ran.

Micky leant over the sink and looked out of the window to the car park below. He saw the dickhead gang still arguing amongst themselves, pushing and shoving one another until Northern George emerged and started threatening them again. Quickly the gang jumped into BMWs and tore off, the sharp screech of tyres confirming their fright and desperation.

Fucking mugs, Micky thought. *Cowards*. And he shook his head and sniffed.

A minute later George came back to the office. He was calmer now but breathing heavily. He slammed the office door and wiped spittle from his lips. The gun, Micky noticed, was back in his possession.

'Just say the word, Boss.' George rubbed the knuckles of his right hand, his gun hand, and looked meaningfully at Tony. Tony was pacing again, his mouth puckered, thinking.

'How sure are we that the Old Bill won't link me to Dal?'

George considered this a moment. 'Can't be one hundred percent,'

'Shit. Fuck!' Tony lashed out at a lamp standing on a nearby table and the thing went crashing to the floor.

'Too late now, but we should've used a different crew. Anyway, I reckon we should put the word out this lot were trying to do a deal behind your back with the Turk. It went bad and that's why they offed him. Nothing to do with you giving any orders. They're young, greedy and disorganised enough that the Filth'll believe it.'

Tony considered this a while. 'I'm not signed up to that one, George,' he sniffed. 'Makes it look like I can't control my own fellas,'

'True, that's a downside. But what's the alternative, Boss? Have the Met all over us? That lot might start flapping their gobs if they get picked up,'

With a sigh, Tony bent down and retrieved the lamp. 'Alright, I hear you.' He set it back in its rightful place. 'Just in case any of them do decide to think about talking, we need to make sure it ain't fucking happening,'

George agreed with a single nod of his head. 'Sure. I'm all over it.' He pocketed the gun again and zipped up his jacket.

'No fuck ups,' he was warned. 'Cut them up, make it look like an Istanbul revenge job,'

'No problem boss,'

'Give me a bell later, yeah? When it's done.'

Now that he had his orders, Northern George left at once to undertake his mission.

Recognising his limited use in the situation, Micky continued to solemnly dry the dishes, but as he did so he thought about the gang and their BMWs. Even useless fuckwits somehow managed to get themselves a shiny new motor or two. Meanwhile he was still stuck with the old Merc. It wasn't right. It wasn't fair. He put the last clean plate away in the cupboard and set about sweeping up breadcrumbs from the floor.

Tired, frustrated and stressed, the boss sank down onto one of the sofas. He sat with his head in his hands and his elbows on his knees. Micky watched him for a while, and felt a strange kind of sadness come over him. Suddenly Tony Vincent looked older than fifty-four. There were grey streaks appearing in his dark hair, and deepening lines around his eyes. This was all a lifetime away from that little boy who liked riding his bike and running around playing soldier out the back of the Toast. With a sigh,

Micky turned, flicked on the kettle, and rummaged in a pot for a tea bag.

When the old man approached and put the hot drink on the table before him, Tony finally lifted his head again. He met Micky's pale grey stare, and then, rubbing his face, snorted out a short, mirthless laugh.

'I bet it weren't like this back in Dad's day,' he said wearily. 'I bet he kept everyone on a short chain.'

Micky cocked his head, thinking.

'Different times,' he said. 'Back then, if you wanted somebody to disappear, they disappeared. For good,'

Tony reached for the mug, nodding. 'I hear you,'

'There weren't none of these half-arsed bodge jobs. You didn't do what needed doing, someone sorted you out, know what I mean? Youngsters today ain't got no bottle, that's the trouble. They ain't got a fucking clue.'

The tea was red hot, but Tony still attempted a sip. He looked up at Micky. He knew all about the old boy's past. He knew what he'd done, what he'd been capable of. 'Yeah, well… things ain't what they used to be,' he mused. 'Finding reliable fellas is a daily struggle in this game. Maybe I need to get myself some more like you, Micky. Not afraid to get their hands *properly* dirty,'

Cut a body into bits, you mean, Micky thought. *Cut it up into so many chunks it'll never be pieced back together again. And then, just to make sure, feed it all to the pigs…*

He blinked slowly at Tony and narrowed his eyes.

'I think you do need someone like me, Boss,' he said, and added just before he shuffled off back into the kitchen: 'Not that you'll find another Micky the Knife, that is.'

The Surgeon of Loughton

CHAPTER FIVE

2016

Fish and chips, smothered in brown sauce and eaten from their paper wrapping, was Micky's dinner that evening. He ate in front of the television for a change, sat hunched up on his sofa, eyes glued to the screen. The smell of vinegar and fried food did its best to overpower the usual sour stink of the room, although Micky was oblivious. He barely tasted the food, chewing methodically but without great interest, for the programme was the thing holding his attention.

It had started innocuously enough: a discussion on whether badgers should be culled to prevent the spread of bovine tuberculosis. Micky had watched, intrigued, wondering if it might positively or negatively affect the supply of badger carcasses in future. The programme finished just as he swallowed the last mouthful of fish, and he then got up and wandered to the kitchen to fetch himself a beer.

As the dying daylight left a faint orange haze over the rooftops opposite, Micky came to stand at the living room window. He eyed his old car. She'd misfired again as he'd tried to start her after leaving Tony's club, and had rattled and hissed like a dying serpent all the way home, Micky urging her on with curses and threats. He was beyond sick of the Mercedes. 'You're on your arse,' he muttered, and swallowed a mouthful of the beer, wincing. It was lukewarm: the fridge in the kitchen was also in its death throes. 'If I had a couple of grand, I'd buy one of those bloody Japanese hatchback things and be done with it,' he told himself sullenly.

Outside, the Merc sat on the driveway, grille facing towards him, giving him a wounded look that seemed to say: *I know you're talking about me. I know what you're planning.*

Micky grunted. Once upon a time he'd been unbelievably proud of that car. He'd driven his friends here, there, wherever they wanted to go. They'd been impressed by the smooth handling, the power, the blue velvet upholstery and walnut finishing. He'd even managed to convince May Vincent to take a ride with him on a few occasions.

May. Micky shifted and looked towards the black and white photo on the shelf. The familiar knotted, painful sensation returned to his guts as he thought of her. That lovely, pale face. The stern look she often had in her eyes. The smell of perfume she left in his car. He could still recall it, even now. Truth be told, he'd bought the 280SEL for her, hoping it would be enough, hoping that she would see him as more than just another face in Charlie's gang. That she would want to spend time with him, just driving around, going places, riding in style. And then coming to trust him, to like him, even to... to...

He closed his eyes and it was the sixties again.

The north-west London streets at night. Driving the Merc through the wet, lamp-lit boroughs, Gene and Debbe playing on the radio, and a smile on his lips. May in the seat beside him, dressed for a night out. Little black velvet gloves covering her hands. She was quietly admiring the car. He looked over at her and grinned.

'This alright for you?' He startled her from her thoughts. She blinked and he added, 'You like it?'

'It's quite nice,'

'Nice?' Eyes widened in mock outrage. 'It's better than nice.' He paused, working out how far he could push things. 'I bought it for you, you know,'

May gave a snort. 'Oh, please.' When she saw Micky's proud expression falter she reached over and prodded his arm. 'Look, you don't have to do those sorts of things to impress me. This car, I mean. It's not necessary,'

He frowned a little, and his eyes darted between her and the road ahead. On the streets, everyone was going places; pavements lined with couples off out to dinner, to dance. None of the women were as pretty or as smart as May, he noticed.

'Are you saying you aren't impressed?'

'I'm saying—,' giving his arm another little tap, '—you don't need to go out of your way for me. An expensive motor like this isn't everything, Micky.' She sat back, wriggling slightly in the seat. Her glance shifted to the side window and the scene beyond. 'It takes more than that to make a decent man.'

In the reflected glow of the streetlights, May's face looked ethereal, and suddenly sad and solemn. It worried him. There was a long pause. The music changed; the Delfonics now. He tightened his grip on the steering wheel. His palms were sweating. He could cut a man from balls to breast with a cool hand, but he couldn't help but perspire and tremble all over when he was with her.

'Come on May, you've gone all serious on me again,' he said softly. She looked at him.

'Sorry,'

'Where does Charlie think you're going tonight?'

'Well... he didn't ask and I didn't tell,'

She must have seen his unease. She undoubtedly shared it, too.

'Micky, I... oh God. Maybe we shouldn't do this,'

These were words he had been dreading, but also half expecting. And in an instant his heart was beating wildly, terrified.

He swallowed, licked his lips. 'You saying you want me to take you back?'

Beside him, May sat twisting her gloved fingers together; nervous, uncertain, not sure what to do for the best.

'Look, if you don't want to go out with me—,' he prompted, nerves still singing with fright.

What if she said she wanted to go home? How could he ever get over the rejection? It had taken long enough just to get her to agree to meet him. Four times he'd sneaked her away right under Charlie's nose, and he wouldn't have taken such a risk for any other woman. She'd warmed to him, but now it felt as though it was all hanging on a cliff edge again.

'It isn't that. You know it isn't that. It's—,'

'Your brother?' His heart trilled in his chest.

May smiled wanly. 'Charlie can be a bit much. A bit intense. And I don't want to get you into trouble,'

'Bit late for that maybe.' A passing car beeped its horn and Micky waved to the driver. He felt May stiffen.

'Who was that?'

'Pal of my old man, God rest him. And not from round your way. He doesn't know Charlie Vincent,' he reassured her.

'Oh. Alright,'

She was still tense, too tense, and he was feeling nothing but bad about it. So he took a deep breath and said, 'Listen May, you coming out with me again, well, I just want to say... it means a lot to me. It really does. But if it's too much grief, I'll understand.' He took his eyes from the road a moment to check her reaction. 'If you want I'll turn around and take you straight back. Just say the word. I want you to have a good time, but if all this just makes you uncomfortable. Well, that wouldn't be right, would it?'

She absorbed his little speech. Kind words, well intentioned. Not something she was used to. Men fawned over and flattered her, but few would put themselves at risk for her. Not the way Micky had. She thought carefully about what he had said, and eventually her shoulders relaxed. She smiled. She reached out and rubbed his forearm again.

'So this place you're taking me to for dinner. What's it like? Not one of Charlie's old haunts is it?'

Micky pulled a face. He tilted his head back and grinned, wide as he could. 'Charlie?' he repeated. 'In Hertford? Not a bloody chance.'

※

Still standing at his living room window, Micky slowly downed the rest of his beer. He stared again at the old Merc on the driveway. The car hadn't been enough, not by a long stretch. He put the bottle down sharply on the window sill and returned to slump on the sofa, dejected, miserable, alone.

The television tried to offer him solace.

'Up next, we hit the roads with Essex County Council to find out how they look after our environment. Keeping the streets clean for over one and a half million residents,'

He rolled his eyes and exhaled loudly.

'Jesus pissing Christ! Is this my life? Is this it?' he railed at the dirty ceiling. It didn't respond. He glared at the TV, annoyed but too lazy to get up, find the remote and change the channel. So the programme played out before him, firing facts and figures at a bemused Micky, things he didn't realise he needed to know. Like how many metal cans were recycled in the county last year. The amount of money spent cleaning up after fly-tippers and illegal dumping. And why landfill costs were rocketing. At least it took his mind off May. Finally, bored beyond belief, he summoned the will to scrabble for the remote control where he'd last seen it, on the floor.

Although... something gave him pause.

Clifton, a so-called Sanitation Officer with a bushy orange moustache and nicotine stains on the fingertips of both hands, was driving his van somewhere Micky knew well: a B-road just north-east of Blackmore Village, heading towards Chelmsford. Clifton was an angular, twitchy man who talked with a curious excitement about his job. It was strangely appealing, and Micky soon found himself listening more attentively. He'd been out that way plenty of times before – not for a long time, admittedly – accompanying men who were on their last ride before they were 'silenced', usually out in the woods or in the middle of Beecher's Lake. There were bodies buried out there that no one else but Micky knew about, that no one else would likely ever find. Burying the unwanted: not something that Clifton would know much about, Micky sniffed.

Yet he was wrong.

On the road that ran alongside Stoneymore Woods, Clifton hopped out from his van and slipped on his protective gloves. *'It's a health and hygiene hazard, you see,'* he explained to the camera as he opened the back of the van and extracted his shovel and a yellow plastic sack. *'Members of the public call us when they spot something on a road, and we go out and collect it. Easy as that.'*

Now he demonstrated his trade. Walking around to the edge of the road, he bent over to scoop up a very dead, very mashed fox with his shovel. Micky made a face. *Terrible waste*, he thought. Next, Clifton slipped the corpse into the yellow bag, twisted it, and fastened it shut with a cable tie. He took it back to the van and tossed it into a large plastic bin. With a gloved hand he held the lid open for the camera to peer inside. *'I've already collected a couple of badgers, some rabbits and a few pheasants today,'* he explained. *'We get a lot of animals killed on the roads out here. It's all rubbish that I need to collect.'*

'Rubbish?' Micky narrowed his eyes at the word. 'It ain't rubbish, you mug! What do you know, eh?'

The camera had cut to a shot of Clifton driving into a secure compound. *'This is it,'* the man grinned. *'This is where we dispose of 'em.'* He was shown backing up his van, slipping out of his driver's seat and opening the rear door. Clifton wheeled the bin filled with roadkill to the edge, and, just like on the refuse lorries that slowly trundled, beeping and reversing, around the streets of every town, settled it into a mechanism that lifted and upended the plastic bin. The contents tumbled out, but instead of falling into a compactor, the yellow bags were deposited straight into the mouth of an incinerator chute.

'Job done,' beamed Clifton, and with a theatrical swipe of his hands he walked off camera.

The programme ended soon after. Micky yawned and rubbed at his eyes. Time for bed, he thought. 'Too much excitement for me.' He heaved himself up, clicked the television off, and shuffled the short distance to the corner of the room. There he sank down onto his old, lumpen mattress with a sigh. At least it would be Saturday in the morning, and he could enjoy his usual fry-up and a day of working on the lamb and the fox. The troublesome Merc could stay on the drive and he could worry about getting someone out to have a look at her on Monday.

He spent a restless night however, searching in vain for sleep. For hour after hour Micky lay, dozing lightly if he was lucky, wide awake and staring into the darkness if he wasn't. His brain, it seemed, wouldn't let him have any peace. It was as though it had some important message to relay to him, some fact or detail it wanted to bring to his attention. But when he gave in and tried to listen to what it had to say, it fell abruptly silent, drawing on random memories from the past and refusing to discuss the present.

Around a quarter to five in the morning, his troublesome mind finally gave in and let him in on the secret.

Invisible fingers prodded him in his half-slumber and immediately Micky jolted awake. He pulled himself up onto one elbow, and, rubbing his face and his sore eyes, he looked out at the room and blinked at the growing daylight.

'That's an idea,' he said to himself, not quite recognising his own voice, strained as it was by lack of sleep. A tremulous bolt of excitement had struck him. 'Micky, you old villain. I think it might just work.'

CHAPTER SIX

1968

Jogging up the Toast Club's rear staircase, Micky the Knife was breathless. It wasn't the exercise that was affecting him, more the thrill, the excitement of seeing May again. As he reached the halfway point he stopped, looked cautiously through the porthole window in the door, and eyed the club.

The bar was to the left. There, Charlie Vincent sat smoking and talking to a couple of his men. A waiter was cleaning tables and another man was sweeping the floors. Otherwise the club was empty. Micky lingered to watch Charlie a moment, to absorb his demeanour. He seemed in a placid frame of mind, nodding and looking satisfied with whatever his workers were telling him. Micky backed away, into the shadows. *Good*, he thought. The boss wasn't in a stinking mood. Whatever he'd summoned Micky for, it wasn't because he wanted to give him a shoeing over May. Breathing more easily, he turned and carried on up the stairs. Charlie could wait for two minutes. First he had another visit to make.

At the door of the flat above, he rapped politely and waited for her to come. He heard voices, a laugh, and then the click of the lock being opened.

May peered out, and seeing him stood there opened the door a few more inches.

'Well, well,' she smirked.

'Sorry 'bout the surprise visit, darlin',' he told her. 'Had to see you,'

Micky reached for his love, attempting to kiss her on the cheek, but her eyes widened and she quickly pushed him away, though with a smile on her lips.

'You're a mental case, Micky. My brother's just downstairs. And I'm in the middle of making Tony his tea,'

With perfect timing, the boy called out to her from somewhere inside the flat. 'Auntie May! Something's burning!'

May rolled her eyes. 'Alright! I'm coming. Don't you touch that stove!' She looked at Micky again. 'I'd better go. What did you come up for anyway? I thought we weren't meeting 'til tomorrow,'

'I had an idea,' he told her, and reached for her again. This time she didn't push him away. 'I didn't want to wait to tell you,'

'Oh God, a man with an idea. Well? What is it?'

'Come away with me this Saturday. We'll go down to the coast. Get out of here for a bit.' His arm snaked around her waist and he pulled her close. 'A mini holiday, just you and me,'

May kept one hand on the edge of the door. She didn't want Tony to see what was happening. In all innocence he might say something to Charlie and then... well, it just didn't bear thinking about.

'What, go off, just like that?'

'Yeah. Just like that,'

Tony again: 'Auntie May!' His little voice growing shriller.

'I'm coming! For crying out loud, Tony!'

Micky didn't release her, though she tried to tug herself back across the threshold.

'So, what do you think?'

'I think you can't be serious. How am I meant to get away from here?' Adjusting the collar of her sweater, she pouted at him. 'There's Tony to look after for a start. What am I supposed to do with him? And what would I say to Charlie?'

'You're making excuses,' he told her.

'Not excuses, *reasons*. And bloody good ones they are, too,'

'I thought we agreed we wanted to keep on seeing each other,'

'Yes, we did. But you can't just expect me to drop everything just to spend a night with you.' Now she was being rational, even cool. 'Just so you can get your leg over,'

May scowled at him. Micky tutted, brushing aside her concerns with a look.

'Listen, I thought I already told you,' he said. 'This ain't just a bit of fun for me. Christ, if it were don't you think I'd have found someone else, some girl who isn't related to Charlie bloody Vincent?'

He paused to lean in and kiss her brow. May's eyes closed and her cheeks began to colour.

'I want us to have a bit more time together, that's all. Away from all this. I thought you wanted that as well,'

He was working her now, playing on her emotions. She knew it but still couldn't resist. She looked at his pale eyes and felt her resolve slipping away.

'I did. I do. It's just—,' she let out a huge sigh and looked to the heavens. 'How am I meant to get away?'

Micky had already considered the problem. He was a criminal after all, and nothing if not inventive. 'Ain't you got a girlfriend getting married, or maybe having a kid? Someone who needs her old friend May to come help out for a couple of days?'

He looked at her meaningfully. Slowly May absorbed the suggestion. It could work. Her face crinkled with a smile. Then she chuckled and slapped his arm.

'You're a bad influence, Micky. A very bad influence. You're corrupting me,'

'Bloody hell I hope so,' he murmured, and he kissed her again, this time tasting her lips and tongue. They stood like that for a long moment until a bawl from inside the flat broke the reverie.

'AUNTIE MAY! Where are you?'

They parted. Micky gave May a look. 'Sounds like a tiger needs feeding,'

She rolled her eyes again. 'Something like that,'

'Just think about what I said, alright? I've got to go see Charlie now but I'll pick you up at eight tomorrow night and we can talk more about it then,'

'Alright.' She stepped back, preparing to shut the door. 'Be careful,'

'Ain't I always?' he said, and blew her a final kiss before he skittered down the stairs.

†

In the club it was the calm before another storm. The dancefloor empty, the band not due for another two hours. Bottles and glasses chinked as the staff stocked up the bar for the night's trade. Micky presented himself to Charlie Vincent, and when the boss was ready he waved away his other minions – all bar one, a huge, muscular man with a suitably brooding expression, who stayed firmly put at Charlie's shoulder.

The boss bade Micky sit with him.

'Michael, my boy.' He inspected him with his hawkish stare. 'Glad you could make it,'

Did he know? Did he suspect? Micky gave him a small nod and settled himself onto the barstool opposite. 'No problem Mr Vincent.'

When Charlie glanced away to pick up a tumbler of gin, Micky dabbed at his mouth, hoping May hadn't left a smear of lipstick there. The swiftest glance at his fingertips settled his nerves: she hadn't.

'I heard you had a job for me,'

Charlie swivelled back towards him. 'I have.' Now the tone was more serious. 'Something important's come up. As per our usual arrangement, I need absolute discretion on this,'

'Of course, Mr Vincent. You know me,'

Charlie raised an eyebrow. 'Indeed I do, Michael. Indeed I do.'

Without the boss saying a word or moving a muscle, the giant at his shoulder suddenly stepped forward, produced a packet of cigarettes, and removed and lit one. Charlie accepted the cigarette, took a quick drag, then blew the smoke into the air above Micky's head.

'It's an urgent job,' he said, in between smoking and sampling the gin. 'And it needs doing this week. One of my business associates has gone and got himself into a bit of a mess. Needs assistance. *Specialist help.*' He pointed the tumbler at Micky. '*Your* kind of help. Need I say more?'

This week. His first thought was, would this interfere with seeing May? But naturally he didn't voice it.

'No, Mr Vincent, I understand,'

'Good. Thought you'd say that. Now,' a nod towards the muscle at his shoulder. 'Eugene here has all the details for you. If there's anything you need, equipment, whatever, you just let him know.' Another swallow and the glass of gin was done. 'Come back and see me when you've sorted out my associate's *difficulties*,'

'I will. As soon as,'

'Good lad. See you around, Michael.'

Charlie turned his head away. Their conversation was done.

With a cold sweat on the back of his neck, Micky followed the beefy monster Eugene out to a store room to receive the more detailed instructions. He'd lived to fight another day, he told himself. But he couldn't carry on like this forever. At some point he'd have to come clean to Charlie and ask him for official permission to see May. At least if he wanted to keep his cock and balls and stay alive.

Micky chewed on his lip and looked up at Eugene. 'Alright,' he nodded at the big man, eager to take his mind off losing his own life. 'Who am I sorting out this time?'

CHAPTER SEVEN

2016

The lamb and the fox were finally finished.

It had taken him the best part of a fortnight, but he was finally happy with his creation. Micky stood in the workshop, hands on hips, twisting his head this way and that, inspecting the mounting with great care. It was one of his best he thought. The lifelike pose of the fox leaping upon the prone lamb, the prey's legs bucking wildly in the air. Expressions of need and desperation on the creatures' faces. Bared teeth and wide eyes. The wet gleam of lips and noses. He'd captured it all. Micky allowed himself a satisfied chuckle. All this, without a single stitch to be seen. The fur of both beasts was immaculate, and showed no signs of ever having been tampered with. It was as though they were still intact, still alive, still fighting one another for survival.

'Bleedin' brilliant, even if I do say so,'

He rubbed his hands together, hardly able to contain his delight.

Less pleasing was the state of affairs with the car. After locking up the workshop, Micky pulled on his overcoat and a small woollen cap and walked to the bus stop at the far end of his street. The Merc had failed him again, perhaps for the last time. When he'd tried to start her the previous day, intending to head over to the supermarket, she'd steadfastly refused to comply. The RAC man who came out had sighed heavily and shook his head as he looked at the old girl, and could only offer to tow her to a specialist.

'They don't make them like they used to,' he'd offered, a small and pointless condolence. Micky had glowered.

'Thank Christ they don't,' he sneered his reply. 'Might as well sell her for scrap.'

Images of a huge, vastly unaffordable repair bill had finally cowed Micky into accepting reality. He'd waved off the RAC man, left the Mercedes on the drive, and resigned himself to catching the bus for the foreseeable future.

At Bar 101, preparations for Christmas were underway. It was late November, and Tony had employed a few new girls to help festoon the club with decorations. As he headed for the stairs up to the office, Micky cast his eye over their lithe bodies clad in tight jeans and ugly boots, and wondered when young women would go back to wearing fitted skirts and heels again. Still, he smiled at the girls and they smiled back.

'Alright, Grandad?' one of them called out.

'Not so bad, Girls, not so bad.'

They laughed at him as he doffed his mucky cap, and a heavy-breasted blonde blew him a kiss. Micky grinned. Then he chided himself silently: *Even forty years ago you were too old for them.* He gave a wistful sigh and hurried off.

Upstairs the office was in darkness. As he pushed open the door, Micky thought for a moment that he'd gotten his days mixed up. He looked around. It was just after ten in the morning according to his watch, and the sky was a thunderous grey outside. All the lights were off, save for a small red LED blinking on Tony's answering machine. Surely it was Wednesday? Micky unbuttoned his coat. He snapped on the lights and started when a movement suddenly caught his eye.

Northern George was lying on one of the sofas. He stirred, stretched and yawned at Micky's interruption, and slowly pulled himself up into a seated position. His callused hands rubbed at his tired, greasy face.

'Jesus wept. What time is it?'

Micky finished taking off his coat and hung it by the door. 'Hard night, was it?' He threw George a disapproving glance. 'Or has the wife kicked you out again?'

George was fully clothed. He'd slept under his leather jacket. It creaked when he moved.

'Don't talk to me about that ungrateful cow.' He yawned again. 'I had some shit to sort out for Tony with those girls up on Tower Street. You'd think slags would know how to make a proper living on their backs. Not that lot. Broke again, the lot of them. Make us a brew, would ya Mick?'

The old man dutifully set the kettle to boil. He was just listening to it begin to simmer, pouring milk into a mug, when he heard the door open.

'Fucking prick!'

Tony Vincent had arrived.

'What's the score, boss?' George was wide awake now, sounding suddenly perky. But Micky heard the cautious note in his voice and looked over his shoulder. He saw Tony stalking over to his desk. For a change he was wearing casual jeans, trainers, and an unflattering sports jacket instead of one of his sharp suits. He looked tired, rough even, as though he too had spent the night on a sofa somewhere. He had a bunch of keys in one hand and he tossed them angrily onto a pile of papers.

'Raymond has fucked us.' He looked at Northern George, whose face was now puckering. 'He's been stealing gear, stealing from *me* and then selling it on to that fat cunt McMahon!' Tony jabbed an angry finger at George. 'I want him dealt with, you know? No fucker steals my shit and gets away with it.'

The blood began to pump a little faster through Micky's veins. He poured the boiling water into two cups, stirred coffee into one and milk and a teabag in the other, and held his breath.

'So what do you want done?'

'I want him gone. Dead!' Tony snarled. 'I don't care if he is my fucking cousin twice removed or whatever the hell it is! Shit, why is my life perpetually invaded by these *cunts?*'

Both Micky and George kept their eyes glued on the angry man. When he was agitated Tony was especially dangerous.

'Things have to be done properly this time,' referring to the botched disposal of the Turk, Burak Dal. Tony glared at George as though it was suddenly all his fault. 'You take care of it personally, you hear me? I've got big deals going down this month. I can't afford the Old Bill crawling all over me.'

George understood. Wordlessly, he got up just as Micky wandered over with the drinks on a plastic tray. George took a huge gulp from his tea, nearly emptying the mug, and set it back down. He pulled on his jacket, looking serious. 'I'll be in touch,' he said to the boss as he left, and then the door banged shut and Tony and Micky were alone.

The old man listened to George's receding footsteps, and felt something akin to little electrical jolts shooting up and down his limbs.

This was it, he knew: the perfect moment. The one he'd been waiting weeks for.

Now Tony was slumped on the sofa, in the warm spot left by Northern George, and glaring at the floor. He seemed to have forgotten the old man was even there. Micky took a breath, put down the tray and licked his lips.

'Tony,' he said, and then again when his boss didn't glance up. 'Tony. Don't mean to disturb you, but I need to have a word,'

A growl of irritation. 'Not now, Micky mate,'

Perseverance. Something he had always believed in. Something he had always had. It had gotten him into Charlie Vincent's gang. It had gotten him into May's affections. Now it was needed to get Tony on side with his plan.

'It's proper stuff,' he insisted. 'Just take two ticks,'

'Seriously, I'm not in the mood. I've got a lot of shit on my mind.' When the old man didn't shift away, Tony looked hard at him. 'Look, call me a prick for saying this, but I ain't got time for whatever it is you want to jaw about. I've got business to sort out.'

To reinforce this point, Tony stood up. His hands went to his hips. But he was too on edge to think clearly, and so he stood there for a moment, looking left and right, checking his phone, his watch but not achieving anything that might have put his mind at ease.

Micky watched him. Perseverance. *Do it now or never,* he told himself. He bit into his lip and shuffled from foot to foot. 'Tony,' he said, 'I think I can help you out with this Raymond fella,'

The proposition drew only a furrowing of the brow from the boss. He didn't even look up from the screen of his phone. 'Eh? What? I don't think he needs a mug of tea, mate,'

'I'm serious Tony. I can help,'

'Yeah I'm sure you think you can, Micky.' Abruptly, he put the phone back into his pocket. 'That's what I have people like George for. He sorts out the shit for me so you can just enjoy retirement,'

Hearing this, the old man looked suddenly defiant, different somehow. Tony hesitated in saying more. He paused and began regarding him carefully, wondering if his father's old retainer had just flipped or whether there was something genuine that he had to offer.

'Alright. Enough with the stare.' He let out a hiss and shook his head. 'I'll humour you for a second. Come on, what is it you think you can do?'

Delight made every muscle in Micky's face quiver. It wasn't the prettiest of sights. 'I can help you get rid of his body. Assuming Northern George has gone out to do 'im in, I mean,'

These words surprised Tony. At first he wanted to give the old boy a mouthful just for having the nerve to come out with such a load of crap. Then he wanted to laugh. Then he looked in his eyes and wondered if he'd really lost it, if he'd had a stroke or gone mental.

'Are you being straight or taking the piss?'

In an instant Micky looked offended. 'You what? I would never take the piss!' He flapped about for a moment, hands jerking, loose fleshy jowls wobbling. 'I respect you as I respected your old man. No joking, Tony. Not on something like this,'

At the sight of Micky's agitation, and fearing he might have a fit there in the middle of the office, Tony raised his hands and tried to placate him. 'Yeah, yeah. Keep your hair on. Fucking Jesus.'

He sat down again. He leant over and scooped up the coffee that the old boy had made him. Too much milk; not up to Micky's usual standard. Tony sniffed and put the cup back on the tray.

'Alright, I'm all ears. What's this amazing plan you've cooked up in that mental old brain of yours?'

At last! Abruptly, Micky plopped down on the sofa beside him. 'Listen boss, I reckon I can get rid of the body,'

'You already said that,'

'No, I mean completely, without a trace. No grave to be found, nothing to wash up on a beach somewhere. Just.... Gone.'

There was a pause whilst Tony Vincent assimilated this information. Little lights of excitement had started to glow in the old man's eyes. 'Come off it Micky,' he said with a laugh. 'You're having me on,'

'No, straight up, boss,'

He leaned a little too close and saw Tony wrinkle his nose at the underlying stink of mouldy clothes and chemicals.

'All I need is for a couple of fellas to deliver the body to my place, very early doors. Course they'll have to get rid of his ID and all that. Oh, and I'll need the body stripped naked.'

Micky waited. He waited and then saw Tony's puzzled face begin to crease as he broke into a loud, strident laugh.

It wasn't what he wanted to hear.

'Fucking hell, mate! What are you planning to do with a naked dead bloke at your age?'

There was no point, Micky knew, in getting defensive. If he wanted to get Tony to sign up to this plan he had to stay determined. He had to show him that he meant business. He had to be like the old Micky again, Micky the Knife. So he gritted his teeth, clenched his fists, and fought back the desire to lash out.

'You don't need to know the details of what I've got in mind,' he told him. 'Leave that all to me,'

Tony continued to guffaw. 'Fuck's sakes,' he spluttered. 'I'll have nightmares tonight, thinking about you alone with Raymond's stiff.' But the laugh died on his lips when he saw how serious Micky still was. 'Are you actually being straight with me?'

"Course I am. You know my form, Tony. You know I can handle this sort of thing,'

'I know you could mate, thirty, forty years ago. Now you make a decent brew but you ain't exactly kept up the old skills, have you?'

The look of wounded pride on the other man's face made Tony regret his harsh words. He sat back, massaged his brow, and exhaled loudly. This day was turning out to be a massive pain in the fucking bollocks. And he hadn't even had any breakfast yet.

After some thinking, he dropped his hands to his thighs and looked at the old man again.

'Alright. Let's say for the sake of argument that I do go for whatever this plan of yours is. No disrespect Micky, but this ain't the sixties. If something goes wrong I can't just pay off the Met and it all goes away. If you get caught – fuck, if I get *implicated* – it'll mean jail time. Big jail time. D'you hear me? At your age that'll be a life sentence and then some,'

Micky bristled. 'I hear ya,' he said stiffly. 'But I ain't afraid of a bit of bird. Never have been,'

'Yeah well, prison ain't what it used to be. You'll be in with any old scum. Rapists, paedos, Pikeys. They won't treat you with the respect Micky the Knife deserves,'

The old man lifted his chin defiantly. 'If that's the way it has to be, so be it,'

'Micky, listen to what I'm saying. I'm trying to talk you out of this. For your own good, not just mine.'

As Micky looked at Tony's dark but greying head, he pictured himself standing in the Toast Club again. He remembered how his knees almost knocked – yes, Micky the Knife, afraid! – as he finally asked Charlie for his permission to take May out on a legitimate date. The answer then had been no. A big fat no. Accompanied by Charlie turning puce and looking like he was about to explode. However, never one to give up that easily, he'd worked on Charlie after that, always proving and reinforcing his worth, until one day he'd asked the question again and the boss had relented. 'You're my man, ain't you Michael?' Charlie had said, and then after peering at him and taking his time to think over the matter for what felt like forever, said, 'Alright, you can take May out.'

Perseverance.

'But no funny business. You take her out, you bring her home. Untouched.' A steely glare. 'You're my man, so you do what I say and I let you have your little fantasy with my sister. As long as you keep your hands and your prick to your fucking self. Understand me, Michael?'

Had he understood? Looking back, he could see now that he hadn't. There had been no comprehension on his part on exactly what deal he had done. He should have known that nothing came for free with Charlie Vincent. But as Micky looked hopefully at Tony, he brushed aside the thought that he might be about to commit the same mistake twice. Instead he prayed that the son would see sense and give him his chance, without asking for a chunk of his life in return.

'All I'm asking-,' said Micky, his voice almost trembling with emotion, '-is to prove myself. Let me prove myself again, Tony. That's all. I might be old but I ain't bloody useless.'

Tony was silent for a long time. His mouth worked as his brain chewed over the options. Finally his eyes narrowed, his jaw relaxed and he began to blink rapidly. He let out a long groan and rolled his eyes to the ceiling. 'For fuck's sakes. I hope I'm not going to regret this,'

A bolt of pure joy tore through Micky's chest then. He clasped his hands together, grinned his lopsided grin and squirmed with delight. Tony eyed him, shaking his head.

'So you're not going to tell me the gory details of this plan?'

'Better if you don't know.' The old man calmed himself enough to get back to his feet, and reached to scoop up the tea tray.

'When would you be ready for delivery?'

'I'm ready now,' shrugging lightly, but proudly. 'Tell George to give me a bell. I will need to know if this Raymond has any metal in him,'

'Eh?'

'Like plates in his skull, pins in his legs. That sort of thing,'

'How the fuck should I know?'

Micky backed away. 'Alright, alright. Just asking. It'll be easier if I know in advance, that's all. Save chipping a blade on the titanium.'

He moved back to the kitchenette, a new liveliness to his gait and a grin on his face. He knew that Tony's eyes remained on him, that he still had doubts, probably dozens of questions. But he didn't mind. *I'll show him soon enough,* he told himself as he tipped the boss' coffee into the sink. *He'll see.*

'This better not be the thing that finishes me off, old man,' Tony called out to him, and Micky, squeezing a blob of green washing-up liquid into the cup, just smiled.

†

The corpse of Raymond, Tony's cousin, arrived a few nights later. Micky was waiting for it, just as planned. He saw the car glide almost soundlessly to a halt at the edge of his driveway, and two men got out. They were both dark-skinned, almost invisible in the shadows of the night. They looked up and down the road, and after a long minute that seemed like an eternity to Micky, watching from his front window, went around to the boot of their car and began hauling something out.

He met them at the gate by the side of the house. Using sign language, Micky silently pointed them to the workshop at the far end of the garden. The men carried the corpse between them, contained inside an enormous holdall. Micky hurried ahead and opened up the workshop, then using only torchlight directed them to the chest freezer.

He lifted the lid and stood back, watching intently as Tony's men unzipped the bag, revealing the body. Rigor had passed. Raymond was of wiry build, though paunchy around the middle. His face and naked torso were livid with bruises, and there was a clear ligature mark around his neck. George's work, no doubt. The men hauled the corpse into the icy mist of the freezer. Micky had already made sure it was empty, ready for this new arrival. When they were done, the two men rolled up their bag and as quietly and discreetly as they'd arrived, they were gone.

Alone in the workshop, Micky stood, clad in his dressing gown and a pair of worn-out slippers, and looked at the head and knees of the man barely poking out through the cold, white fog.

'Now you can show 'em you've still got what it takes,' he whispered to himself, and with a firm clunk he shut the lid.

CHAPTER EIGHT

2016

The next thirty six hours were some of the longest and most dangerous of Micky's life. He stayed at home and watched the street for anything unusual. He was confident the middle-of-the-night delivery hadn't been seen by his neighbours, but be couldn't be completely sure. If for some reason someone did report suspicious goings on, it wouldn't take much of a search for the Old Bill to turn up Raymond's frozen corpse hidden in his freezer.

Yet as the hours passed Micky grew in confidence. No flashing lights and screaming sirens disrupted his peace, and eventually he decided the time was right. He took a rare bath, dressed himself in clothes he could easily burn, and headed up to the workshop with a pile of sandwiches and his expression set in grim determination.

The approach he took was simple. Using his circular saw and a set of sharp new blades, Micky set about cutting up Raymond into smaller, more manageable pieces. The frozen meat and bone was easier to handle than raw, since it produced very little mess. And the neighbours would hardly think twice about Micky using his power tools in his workshop. So he was left undisturbed.

It took over two hours to separate the body into the requisite chunks. Afterwards, Micky stacked them more neatly in the freezer, separating each one with sheets of newspaper, then carefully washed down and disinfected his tools with all due care. Finally, he helped himself to a round of sandwiches before he set to work on the badger.

He had a plan, a very definite one. 'You have to be cautious,' he told the dead animal as he attended to it, emptying its putrefying guts into a pail on the bench. 'Start small, then work up to the big stuff. I mean, if you've never done something before you have to check that it's all *feasible*. You need to know you're not going to make a right tit of yourself, get something wrong and end up running from the Filth, or someone worse.'

Badger eviscerated, Micky went to the freezer, opened it, and selected a piece of meat. He took a chunk of the dead man's frozen lower leg, from just below the knee to the bottom of the calf, and returned to the workbench. The selection fitted quite neatly inside the animal. Micky smiled and nodded to himself.

'Like it fucking grew there.'

He packed out the space around the section of leg with some of the badger's own organs, then set about sewing the belly back up. It took patience to ensure the seam could not be noticed without a very close and thorough inspection, but in that respect Micky was an expert. When done, he carefully checked his work and, satisfied, allowed himself another congratulatory sandwich and a cup of tea.

A deer was next. A female Muntjac, a victim of hit-and-run on the Colchester bypass. It was missing a leg, but Micky, for once, wasn't concerned about that. After the organs were removed there was sufficient room for

Raymond's head, and again he set to sewing up the wide incision with all the diligence of a surgeon and all the desire for perfection of an artist.

By late afternoon the work was done. After wrapping the animals in tarpaulin, he put them into a wheelbarrow and took them out to the driveway. There, parked behind the beached Mercedes, was a dark red Vauxhall estate. Micky unlocked it and casually began loading the cargo. The most difficult part of the operation so far had been finding a car hire company that would rent a vehicle to a man of his age, even one with a clean licence. He'd decided not to ask Tony for the loan of a motor; his boss was already twitchy enough about the whole thing going wrong. No, he didn't want to give Tony any cause to change his mind about letting him handle this disposal. This was going to work. It had to.

He paused and sniffed the air. The darkening sky was glowing with the last of the pale, wintry sunset, and he could smell on the air that somewhere close by someone was burning up a bonfire. Micky patted the wrapped carcasses of the deer and the badger. 'You lot'll be roasting away soon enough,' he chuckled as he shut the boot and locked them in.

The test run would be tomorrow.

The Surgeon of Loughton

CHAPTER NINE

1968

Handwell's the butchers on Lower Mill Lane was a place famous for its kidneys and pig's trotters. It had serviced the community in Woodford since the early 1800s, and the Handwells had made such a grand living out of their one little shop that they now lived in a big Edwardian mansion on The Drive in South Woodford.

Of course not everyone knew exactly how the Handwells had made all of their money. Selling giblets and sides of beef to the locals was one income. But old Mr Handwell, current head of the family and still going strong at ninety-three, was as wise and wily as any of his forbears, and as long as Charlie Vincent kept putting business his way from all the restaurants he had dealings with (not that Charlie would ever eat anything that came out of Handwell's shop. He knew better than that), Mr Handwell continued to grant Charlie certain freedoms – for a tasty backhander – when it came to the use of his cold store and butchery room.

That night was one such occasion. Long after the shop had closed to the general public and Handwell's two sons and their assistant had locked up and gone home to roast dinners and warm wives, Micky and his associates pitched up.

Micky knew the place well. He knew where the Handwells left the spare key to the back door, and he also knew how to operate all the mincing, crushing and bone-grinding equipment that they kept for preparing the meat and for disposing of the unwanted parts.

In the tiled butchery room, with the shutters drawn over the windows and one man standing guard by the door, Micky, clad in overalls, was hard at work. It was two days before Christmas, and there he was, dissecting flesh from bone, limbs from torso, and slopping some stupid sod's innards into buckets. Another man, Dennis, a little older than Micky but not high on Charlie's list of friends due to an accident he'd had when chauffeuring Charlie, Tony and May to Mass one Sunday, was in charge of feeding the dead victim's bones into the industrial crushing machine. A fourth man, with a thick Irish accent no one could understand, had the job of hauling buckets of minced human meat into a small furnace, which he did whilst retching constantly.

A fresh bucket of guts was passed to the Irishman by Dennis. The former responded by promptly throwing up all over the tiled floor. Dennis swore at him.

'Fucking useless Paddy cunt,'

'Leave him be,' said Micky, frowning as he cut through a particularly tricky part of what was left of the dead man's hip joint. 'Not everyone has a stomach for this kind of work,'

A neatly-flayed foot went into the bone-crusher. 'You don't say,' Dennis muttered when the machine's grinding roar had died down. It spit out a red and white mash into a container, which the Irishman reluctantly came to collect.

'How the hell do you stand it all day, Mick?' he asked, wincing as Micky roughly manipulated the stubborn joint.

'I don't do it all day. I do it when it needs to be done. Someone has to,'

There was a loud clicking and a popping sound as the hip was worked free. Micky grunted with the effort, then dropped the leg onto the cutting surface.

'Pass me that saw, Den,'

The surgeon set to work on the bloodied leg, hewing it into several parts. When Dennis reached for one of the chunks, Micky stopped him with a hand. 'Don't put the hip bones through that thing. It made the fucker seize last time. And we ain't got time to piss around trying to fix it,'

'Yeah, and I'm not putting my hand in to unblock it,' said the man by the door. 'Nearly lost an arm in it once,'

Dennis shrugged. 'Suit yourselves. But we have to get rid of it all somehow,'

'I know a few places where we can dump a few bits.' Now Micky was sweating as he put his weight behind the saw. 'Christ, this bastard's hard work,'

Dennis was selecting his next piece for the bone-crusher. 'He's a cold fuck, the boss, ain't he?' he observed above the din of the machine. 'Does he tell you how he wants 'em done? How to cut 'em up and all that?' He shook his head, whistling through his teeth. 'If he does, he's a bloody nutter. Mental,'

The man at the door and the Irishman exchanged glances.

'You don't want Charlie hearing you said something like that,'

'Yeah,' agreed Micky. 'He doesn't much like being called a nutter. Can't think why,'

'Especially not when you're already in the shit with him, Den,' muttered the Irishman, in between spewing his guts up. 'I heard about you driving his Jag into the back of the Reverend's Mini at church. Charlie had to be pissed about that,'

Micky paused to wipe the sweat from his brow with his sleeve. The stink of blood, shit and guts had long since ceased to faze him. Now it was just part of the background stench of his life. He tossed another chunk of human meat over to Dennis.

'It was an accident, pure and simple. Could have happened to anyone,' Dennis said defensively. 'Bloody old fool slammed his brakes on at traffic lights, didn't he? I had nowhere to go 'cept straight up his bleedin' Aris,'

'Not a good move, not with the boss in the back of the car,' sniggered the man at the door.

'Yeah well, accident or not, watch what you say about Charlie Vincent.' Micky was back to filleting flesh from bone. 'He hears something he don't like, it might be your head goes through that damned thing next,'

Dennis looked at the bone-crusher. 'More likely your balls, you mean,' he said slyly.

Micky's knife missed a beat. He shot the other man a dark glance. 'You what?'

Part of a fibula screeched and rattled through the machine, and a spray of bone-meal hit the floor.

'I heard you were seeing his sister. He can't be happy about that,'

Eyes narrowed, Micky put down the knife and picked up the saw. 'Not that it's any of your fucking business, but I recently had a word with Mr Vincent about courting May. And he's given me his blessing,'

Murmurs of surprise echoed around him.

'His blessing? Has he now?' said Dennis. 'Well he must be mellowing. I heard the last fella tried it on with May

Vincent ended up floating like a turd in the Limehouse Cut.'

He sniffed, eyed his quarry closely, and tipped a wink at the man standing guard. Then his gaze fixed upon Micky once more.

'You fucked her yet?'

With lightning speed, Micky the Knife dropped the saw, snatched up a severed foot, and flung it, full pelt, at Dennis' head.

†

In the men's room at the Toast, Micky stood in front of one of the basins adjusting his tie whilst revellers jostled in and out, all happy, all half-cut, starting the Christmas celebrations with gusto. He'd finished the clear-up with the boys at Handwell's just over an hour and a half ago, and there had been barely enough time to get home to his flat, bathe and scrub himself clean of the blood and the stink of it, and get dressed for the night out. Beneath his suit his skin still felt a little raw. Micky swiped a comb through his hair, smoothing it carefully into place, and for the umpteenth time checked his fingernails again to make sure there were no tell-tale traces there of the victim's blood.

The bathroom door continued to swing open and shut as men came and went, but eventually there was a lull in the comings and goings. Finding himself alone, apart from one guy noisily farting and shitting in the end cubicle, Micky dove into one of his pockets and pulled out a small box. Inside lay a fine gold bracelet: a present for May. He hoped to give it to her that night. He'd dithered about buying it, thinking she might refuse to accept anything that might upset Charlie's delicate sensibilities, but then finally thought sod it and took the plunge. He'd been careful to select something subtle, and since he'd seen May wear a similar one on nights out thought that at least it wouldn't overtly catch her brother's hawk eye.

'It's not like I've bought her a bloody diamond ring,' he muttered to himself. The box snapped shut.

From the cubicle, above the rising stink of fresh shit, the unseen man called out, 'You talking to me there, chum?'

Pushing back out into the club, Micky found the atmosphere to be its usual loud, boisterous but cheery self. The dancefloor was full. Festive decorations hung from every wall, all the mirrors, and down from the ceiling. Scanning the room, Micky's eyes hunted for May. He found her standing with a small group of wives and girlfriends, her dark hair piled up in a mass of curls, and her body cocooned in a slim-fitting fancy white dress covered in a print of red roses.

As though sensing his gaze was upon her, she looked over her shoulder and her eyes met his.

May smiled. Micky grinned. He started the arduous process of elbowing and bumping his way through the packed club towards her. Every step, he kept his eyes on his girl, and made faces as members of the drunken crowd pushed him this way and that. May watched and laughed at his predicament.

A sudden crash of glass and furniture made her start and he saw her head snap round to the right. Following her glance, Micky could see only a whirl of suited arms above the heads of the dancing crowd now swallowing him up. He couldn't tell what was really going on. Yet catching another glimpse of his sweetheart, he noticed that her brow had furrowed. She looked suddenly tense. All the women around her were craning their necks to get a better look at the fracas, and it was clear that something was happening.

Someone bumped up against Micky's ribs. He felt the hard edges of the jewellery box sink into his flesh and he glared at the nearest face. How difficult was it to walk a few bloody paces? Grunting in annoyance, he kept on pushing through the crowd, but when he emerged at the other side, May had vanished.

At the same time, Charlie Vincent entered by the door at the side of the bar. He'd heard the row break out, and with an ear finely-tuned to the sounds of men getting out of order in his club, knew he had to get on top of things before it all got out of hand. After all, the Toast wasn't just a place where people came to drink and dance; it was where most of his big and illicit business deals went down. He couldn't afford for the Old Bill to turn up on the pretext of sorting out some annoying little punch-up and then start sticking their noises into anything else that might be going on.

So with three of his heaviest lieutenants, the fearsome Eugene included, Charlie stalked towards the scene of trouble with his eyes narrowed and his jaw set hard. People got out of his way when they saw him approach. By now the fight had escalated to more than just a few drunken punches being thrown. A table was overturned; glasses and alcohol went flying. Women were shrieking and it was obvious this dispute, whatever the hell it was about, wasn't going to end quietly.

With a flick of his head, Charlie set his hounds loose on the troublemakers. They turned out to be two men, both drunk, both in their twenties. One was already in a bad way: cut eyebrow, burst lip, his face and the front of his suit covered in blood and swaying on his feet like a boxer about to hit the canvas. Two of Charlie's men dealt with him swiftly; a little more roughing up, and then he was dragged out of the club and tossed onto the frozen pavement outside.

The second was more difficult to subdue. From the way he threw up his fists and spat at Charlie's men it was clear he was real source of all the trouble. Charlie stood and watched impatiently as the muscular Eugene grappled with the man. Despite his intoxicated state he was nimble, and didn't mind ducking out of reach behind a woman or two when Eugene tried to grab him by the throat. As people scattered and tried to clear away from the fight, Eugene finally got a grip on the drunk. But a couple of hard smacks to the gut still didn't stop him from running his mouth.

'Hey,' the man slurred, spraying Eugene with a mouthful of blood. 'Why doesn't the old bastard come and have a go at me himself, eh? Why should you do all the hard work for him?' He coughed and spat more red onto the vast breast of Eugene's white shirt. Then his eyes slid sideways to glare at Charlie. 'Look at him, standing there with a stick shoved up his arse. Yeah, you, you useless old cunt!' he hollered. 'Come on, Charlie Vincent! Show me what you've got!'

He didn't say any more. He couldn't, as Eugene had locked his meaty forearm around his neck.

Watching this, watching the crowd, the many pairs of eyes now looking on with shocked fascination, Charlie's face began to redden.

He couldn't let this pass.

'Eugene, bring that bastard to me.'

He flicked his head again and now Eugene was hauling his captive across the floor, towards the bar. With one great foot he kicked open the door to the stairs and the two of them, followed by a seething Charlie, disappeared through it. At the doorway Charlie paused to glance over his shoulder. His eyes zeroed in on Micky the Knife, stood at the edge of the dancefloor. He waited for Micky to notice his steely gaze and then silently summoned him over.

Out in the stairwell, things were not looking good for the drunken idiot. Powered by whisky, he was still struggling against Eugene's superior bulk and strength, hissing curses and trying to spit at Charlie.

'You wanted my attention?' Charlie snarled, voice like ice. 'Well, you sorry little shitbag, you've got it now,'

'Fuck you, you old nonce,' the man managed to rasp. He was on the threshold of passing out. 'Fuck... Charlie... fucking... Vince—,'

He didn't get to say another word. Not one. Not when he saw the knife and Charlie started hacking at his chest and guts with the short blade. Even Eugene was taken by surprise. Three stabs into the boss' blood frenzy, Eugene released the drunk and stepped back, watching with surprise as the older man kept on stabbing, hewing at his victim. When Charlie was done, which took only a matter of seconds, the stairwell and both men were covered in blood. The scene looked like a slaughterhouse, and the drunken brawler was dead.

Charlie stood, breathing raggedly, as though he'd just fought five rounds in the ring.

'Call me a cunt?' he rasped over the seeping corpse. 'Call me, Charlie Vincent a fucking *cunt*?'

The door to the club swung open and Micky stood there, staring in. As soon as he saw the quantity of blood he slid inside the stairwell and slammed the door shut at his back.

'What the fuck—,' he started to say, then saw the warning look that Eugene shot him. Micky's glance moved swiftly to the knife still tight in Charlie's fist. Say the wrong thing now, the big henchman was telling him silently, say *anything* and chances are he'll fucking do you, too.

With great caution, Micky dared look out through the porthole window back into the club. Things were still in disarray. The waiters were trying to clear up the mess and people were standing around, discussing what had just happened. *A fight that got out of hand, nothing else*, he imagined he would say when he went back inside to find May. He glanced again at Charlie. He couldn't let her see her brother like this. The boss was staring down at the dead man; staring at him as though in some sort of trance, with mouth open, lips wet, eyes wild and reddened.

'Shit,' muttered Micky under his breath, and he sensed Eugene tensing. 'Shit.'

At Micky's back there was a hammering on the door. One of Charlie's men wrenched it open and shoved his head around it. In a second he took in the blood-streaked walls and the man lying prone on the floor. He paled but still managed to hiss: 'Someone called the Old Bill. They're coming up the front stairs!'

The man was gone in a flash. Micky and Eugene exchanged glances.

'Mr Vincent, we need to get you out of here,'

Eugene hovered at Charlie's shoulder. But the boss didn't move. He still had the knife in his hand. The big man looked to Micky for help. Reluctantly, Micky stepped forward and tugged at Charlie's jacket sleeve.

'Boss, this is serious. The Old Bill are on their way,'

Slowly, like a man waking up from a daydream or rising from a coma, Charlie lifted his head. He blinked, looked around at the others, and then down at the man on the floor. Finally he raised the hand holding the knife and stared at it, as though he'd never seen such a thing in his life.

There was more of a commotion in the club now. The police were probably inside, scattering and panicking the patrons. They could hear women squealing and male voices shouting. This was more than enough for Eugene. It seemed as though Charlie was docile now, so he grabbed the boss by one arm and started dragging him down the stairwell.

'We're going – now!'

Charlie didn't resist. He let Eugene lead him away.

For a moment Micky was torn. If he went back into the club to find May, he'd risk being scooped up. His shoes had enough blood on them just from standing there to make him a suspect.

If the police spot that, I'll be right in the shit...

He didn't need to think any more. He set off after Charlie and Eugene.

One step, two, four – and then Charlie froze. He turned, looked up at Micky who was just behind him. His dark eyes glittered with something strange.

'Mr Vincent—,' Micky began, and then he yelped as Charlie thrust the knife at him. He threw up his hands. He thought he might be about to die.

But things weren't that simple.

With his empty hand, Charlie Vincent grabbed hold of his arm. 'You're my man, Michael,' he rasped at him, and his breath was hot and acrid in Micky's face. 'Remember? You agreed. You're my man. You have to do what's necessary.'

He pushed the knife, side on, against Micky's open palm and clasped it there, eyes wide, face so close to his that Micky could see that Charlie's pupils were dilated and black, endlessly so, like pools in Hell. The shouting in the club was getting louder. He heard a police siren. And still Charlie stared at him.

'You're my man, Michael. You're my man,'

'Come on!'

With a harsh jerk of his shoulder, Eugene pulled Charlie away. As he did so Micky's fingers folded loosely over the knife. He held it limply and stood watching in a daze as Eugene got Charlie to safety. As they ran down the stairs and left the club via the rear exit. As they fled from the scene. There was the bang of doors. The sound of running feet. Seconds later Micky heard the distinctive note of the Jaguar's engine starting, and then the screech of tyres as the car tore away. Charlie Vincent was gone, but he, Micky...

There was a sudden roaring in his ears. A sound like a wild ocean, like wind whipping up the sea. It was the blood pounding in his head. Dizzily, he turned and slowly walked on leaden legs back up to where the dead drunk still lay. As the police swarmed into the stairwell, shouting and threatening, they found Micky the Knife stood over the man, the weapon in his hand and blood smeared over his palm. Several constables grabbed him, whilst another wrestled the blade away, though he hardly put up a fight. He was shoved onto his knees. Held tight, a hand gripping him by the back of the neck. Others restraining his arms, his torso.

This was it, he knew. This was the price Charlie demanded he pay for seeing his sister.

Someone held the door open and Micky managed to look up, peering through the mass of legs and shouting coppers, and when he did he saw her. She was standing by the bar, looking in. The fright on her pale face instantly turned to terror when she noticed all the blood, and him, Micky, in the middle of it.

The last thing he saw before the constables began smashing their truncheons across his back was May Vincent falling to her knees and screaming.

CHAPTER TEN

2016

'Essex County Council, Waste and Sanitation Department. Julia speaking. How can I help you?'

He pressed the new and unfamiliar mobile phone close to his mouth. 'Hello. I want to report some road kill,'

'Road kill?'

The woman on the end of the line paused a moment and Micky's heart shot up into his mouth.

'You mean, there's a dead animal that needs collecting?'

He almost laughed with relief. 'Yeah, yeah, that's right, that's what I meant,'

'Alright. Can you tell me where the animal is please, Sir?'

'There are two, love,'

'Oh. Two?'

'A badger and a deer. They're about fifty metres apart on the Ridgeway Road, halfway between Stapleford Abbotts and the golf course,'

The sound of typing in the background. Micky listened, wondering if the woman on the phone could hear his pounding heartbeat. He picked at his teeth with a fingernail.

'I've logged that for you now, Sir,' said Julia briskly. 'We aim to collect everything within twelve to twenty four hours,'

What? He froze. This wasn't in the plan.

'Twenty four hours?'

'Yes Sir. That's our standard response time,'

Micky glanced at the clock on the dashboard of the Vauxhall. Twenty-five to three. His mind raced. 'The schools'll be kicking out soon, sweetheart. You want little kiddies to see the animals lying dead on the road, do ya?'

The woman coughed then said, sounding bored, 'Well no, of course not—,'

'They're in a bit of a bad way. Not the sort of thing you want five or six year olds to see,' he went on. Micky listened and heard more clicking of nails on a keyboard.

'Alright,' said Julia. 'I've added a note for the operatives. There aren't many jobs on today, so they might be there fairly soon. I can't promise anything though,'

'You're a star,' Micky told her. 'I appreciate your help, love.'

Before he could annoy her any further, she said: 'Thanks for calling,' and then promptly hung up.

Micky put down the phone. Soon, she'd said. Well it wasn't ideal but it would have to do. He stared ahead. The road was reasonably quiet, mostly straight, built no doubt over an old Roman track. Earlier he'd driven by and when no cars were around, had laid out the two beasts, being careful to place them more on the verge than on the tarmac. He didn't want them to be hit and split open by passing traffic. That would be a fatal mistake. When all this was achieved he'd spun his hire car around and parked up in a little potholed layby to watch what happened.

But how long would he have to wait? He had enough experience of the local Council to know you couldn't rely on a promise they made. What if 'soon' turned out to be twelve hours? Longer?

He sighed and shrugged. Oh well, nothing to be done.

On the passenger seat was a picnic lunch he'd bought at a garage back in Loughton, plus the Daily Mirror and a bunch of old copies of a taxidermy magazine he'd stolen from the library.

'Well at least I came prepared.'

Micky picked up the newspaper and settled down to wait.

†

A couple of hours passed. He finished off all the food, read the paper and one of the magazines, and watched the traffic come and go. He looked at the drivers as they sped by. All oblivious, he thought. All snug and secure in their cars, in their little lives. They knew nothing of the world he'd inhabited. Of the dirty deals, the danger, and of course the violence. The old man glanced at his hands. They looked normal enough: brown liver spots and deep creases on aged, sallow skin. But he'd killed with those hands. He'd cut throats, snipped off fingers, toes and other body parts. He'd helped dig graves and even dunked a man's head and shoulders into a bubbling vat of hot tar (a particularly horrible death). Any normal person would be horrified by that, he knew. But that was the life he'd been born into, a child of the tough East End with no chance of a fancy job and a big house in the countryside. That's how it was, how it was meant to be. Micky glanced at himself in the rear-view mirror. The eyes of an old man, not the eyes of a deranged killer, stared back at him. He wondered for a moment if it might have been different if he'd found himself a woman other than May; a woman on the outside, not involved in Charlie Vincent's world. Could he, perhaps, have settled into a normal life with someone? Could he have turned his back on all of this?

With an impatient tut, Micky re-boxed these thoughts. All were too painful, too distracting. He glanced down at the phone on the seat beside him. He was very tempted to switch it back on and call Tony, to let him know that the first pickup was underway. But he knew he couldn't. Hanging around the boss' office, he'd heard plenty of talk from the young lads about how using your mobile phone could get you a prison sentence. You had to be careful, use only disposable pay-as-you-go phones to cover your tracks, and be sure to ditch them regularly. You could also never switch your phone on at the scene of any badness. The coppers could track you that way.

Micky left the phone where it was and stared intently at the road. If by some chance the parts of Raymond's body were found amidst the animal remains before being turned to ash at the incinerator, it wouldn't be inconceivable that some bright detective could link his call to the council and a subsequent call to Tony, and then all Hell would be set loose. No, he had to wait. He could always tell Tony in person how things were going.

Just as he was beginning to wonder whether he would have to sit up all night or scoop the deer and badger up and start the process all over again the following day, he caught a glimpse of a white, red and yellow van heading towards him in the distance.

'Hello.' His heart gave an excited flutter.

The van driver seemed to be in no great hurry to get to the spot. Micky watched him, anxiously gnawing on his lip and willing the man to *get a fucking move on*. Eventually the vehicle drew up, revealing the familiar livery of the Essex coat of arms, and swung over to the side of the road close to the first animal's remains.

'Here we go.'

The driver hopped out. He was young, in his twenties, dressed in grey overalls edged with fluorescent strips and tied about his waist, with a dark t-shirt above. The driver glanced casually up and down the road, clocking both dead creatures. Micky, a safe distance away in the layby, was of no consequence, and the council worker didn't even seem to notice him.

The man walked over to the badger first, nudging it with his boot before disappearing around to the back of his van.

Micky's pulse quickened. 'Come on, come on.'

The worker reappeared, plastic bag in hand.

'Yes, that's it. Get on with it.'

He watched the little scene play out before him, just as he'd prayed it would. Without bothering to use a shovel, the young man pulled on a glove and lifted the badger into the sack. He then sauntered over to the deer. Again the animal was engulfed in plastic, albeit a little roughly. Micky blanched.

'Christ almighty! Watch what you're doing, you useless prick!'

Safely contained at last, the animals were carried back to the van. Micky heard the dull thuds of the corpses as they were both slung into a container. Moments later the van drove past Micky's car, the driver lighting a fag with one hand as he passed the Vauxhall, before vanishing merrily into the distance.

It was done.

The old man sat still for quite a while, his hands on the steering wheel, just staring ahead at the now empty places where he'd laid the animals to rest.

So far, so good. The plan was working. Micky the Knife tilted his head back, closed his eyes, and allowed himself a smile.

CHAPTER ELEVEN

1971

The visitors' room in HMP Wakefield was only a four-minute walk from Micky the Knife's cellblock, but it may as well have been a thousand miles away.

Since his conviction, no one from the East End had wanted to make the trip all the way up to Yorkshire just to see him shackled and miserable. Old pals and associates thought it best to lay low, usually in fear of being arrested since some were wanted men and keen to stay out of prison. As for Charlie Vincent, there was never any possibility that he would think it right and proper to go see Micky himself, even though he was the man responsible for his incarceration.

Sometimes, when Micky would lie on his bunk at night and examine the minute fissures and cracks in the painted brickwork of his cell wall, he would think about Charlie and May, and his emotions would flick incessantly between rage and misery. Locked up, it was easy to feel victimised. Here he was, doing the boss' time, the rest of his life uncertain. All that had been good in his world, all the possibilities for the future, had been ripped from his grasp by Charlie Vincent. From the moment he'd been arrested May had been lost to him, and there didn't seem any way to get her back. Besides, he told himself in his more pitiful moments, what woman in her right mind would want to be with him? He was a killer and a criminal. He deserved everything that the law could throw at him.

What he got for being 'Charlie's man' was a sentence of fifteen years for voluntary manslaughter. Only a particularly vigorous Brief and a few bribes in the right places had saved him from a murder charge, but there was no avoiding going down. Micky swallowed the punishment. Fifteen years: he'd be in his thirties when he got out. Time enough to start again, to put the past behind him...

Wasn't it?

The first year was the hardest. No visitors, no letters. And nothing at all from May. Weeks and months ticked by and he slowly convinced himself that things had worked out for the best. She was better off without him. When he weakened – which he did occasionally – and began to pine for her again, he would remind himself of all the terrible things he'd done, and then his heart would re-harden. Yes, it had all worked out for the best. She could get on with her life and he... well, he could settle down to the sour, lonely truth of his existence as a convicted criminal.

But one day she finally made that two-hundred mile journey north. And Micky found himself being led down to the visitors' room wearing his prison-issue black boots and blue shirt and trousers. At the door, heart almost thumping out of his chest, he was searched and then nodded through into the room.

His eyes narrowed as he scanned the two rows of tables, searching for her. She wasn't hard to find. Even in a dull brown raincoat with a scarf pulled over her dark hair and her back to him, he easily keyed upon May. Now his feet felt like lead as he approached her table. She turned slightly as she heard his footsteps, and then he found himself looking into that pale beloved face again, and his heart fairly cracked.

Unable to speak at first for fear he would simply scream and wail and not be able to stop the tears, he shuffled into the seat opposite his love and pretended to be more interested in glaring at the nearby guards than in looking at her.

'Hello Micky.'

Her voice was faint, thin, as though it had been stretched and worn through over time. He risked a glance in her direction.

'Alright May.' An enormous lump in his throat. 'Wasn't expecting to see you,'

She looked at him, concerned, fearful. 'How are you?'

'Could be better. Could be worse,'

He shrugged. Inside something was screaming at him. *Wake up! Act like a decent fucking human! Tell her how you feel!* Yet he couldn't do it. He was too afraid of what might happen if he did.

'You look good. Too good for this place,'

She sighed. She was wearing black suede gloves. He remembered riding in the car with her and how she always wore gloves on a night out.

'How's the boy, how's Tony?'

'Oh he's fine.' She sniffed. 'Well, he's as naughty as ever, you know?'

Somehow keeping the acid out of his tone, he said, 'Yeah. Takes after his old man,' and then wondered: did she know? Did she know how Charlie had made him take the fall for killing the drunk?

When she didn't respond directly to his remark he thought he had his answer.

'How are you doing in here? It looks like you've lost a bit of weight.'

'Nah. Still about the same. I ain't got the benefit of a tailor in here, see.' He tugged briefly at his loose shirt. 'Have to make do with what they give me,'

May nodded, appraising him. 'You always looked good in your suits. Always very smart. Charlie says if you want anything, to write him and let him know.'

She smiled, though her mouth trembled as she did so. As Micky looked at her he saw her face crumple and tears glimmered in her eyes.

'May. Jesus—,'

Before he realised he'd done it, he'd reached out instinctively and clasped one of her gloved hands.

'Oi! Enough of that!' A screw shouting from the side. 'No physical contact!'

Slowly, Micky withdrew back to his side of the table. He looked over his shoulder and shot a dark look at the prison officer.

'I'm sorry.' May was fumbling in her coat pocket for a handkerchief. He saw a bundle of several come out at once, all creased and tangled together. Clearly she'd been doing a lot of crying on the journey up.

'Don't upset yourself, sweetheart,' he told her, feeling all the steely resolve that he'd built up begin to melt away, second by second. 'Look, this place ain't somewhere you should be,'

'But I had to come,'

'No. No you didn't,'

She wiped her face. Her eyes were now red. 'Yes I did, Micky. I've put it off for long enough already.' Smoothing back a lock of hair that had escaped from under her scarf, she glanced around self-consciously. 'There's... I've something I wanted to tell you,'

'Couldn't you have stuck it in a letter, something like that?

'No.' A vehement shake of her head. 'No. Not this.'

He took a breath and swallowed it slowly. Whatever this was, it didn't sound good.

There was a long, tense silence between them. All around, the other prisoners and their visitors chattered on. Some even sounded happy. Glad to be reunited, however briefly. But not Micky the Knife and his bird.

May was struggling with herself.

'Fucking hell girl,' he leaned a little towards her over the table. 'Spit it out and put me out of my misery, will ya?'

He meant it to sound light-hearted – though God alone knew why – but it only made May's face twist and she started to cry again. She near smothered herself with the bundle of handkerchiefs, and then suddenly decided Micky was right: out with it, or choke on it.

'Micky. I... I wanted to tell you...'

A hesitation, an enormous gulp of air.

'Micky, I'm getting married.'

Now, instantly, he regretted pushing her to speak. Hearing her announcement, it felt as though something had hacked its way inside his chest and was literally tearing his heart in two. An indescribable pain began sawing through the organ, making him recall the time he'd dished out another punishment on Charlie's orders; cutting through the right arm of a fella whilst the poor sod was still conscious. Micky sat, frozen in agony, mouth sagging as she went on, telling him that she didn't expect he'd be happy about it, and how he might not understand, but that she knew she had to tell him, in person, face to face. He didn't really hear any of it, however. All he heard was the door to the secret room he'd kept in his heart, where he stored his last ounce of hope, being brutally kicked open, smashed to pieces, and the contents within utterly destroyed.

Somehow, at some point, he heard himself ask her questions: 'When...?' and, 'Who...?'

She was still sniffing, wiping her nose now, smearing her make-up a little bit but looking brighter. 'You don't know him. His name's Graham. He works for an insurance company. We're getting married in August. He's taking me to France for the honeymoon.'

May stopped herself. She realised she'd babbled on, given him information he didn't need, possibly couldn't handle, not given his situation. Now her face flooded with the heat of shame.

'I'm sorry, Micky, I really am,'

He was staring at a spot on the table, somewhere just beyond May's gloved hands. For a while he said nothing. When he did speak his voice sounded very small.

'You had to do what's right for you, girl,' he said. 'I've only done a year and a half. You can't wait around for me. It wouldn't be right,'

'Micky—,'

'No.' He shifted in his seat. 'Let me finish.' Now he risked looking at her again, though he confined his gaze to her mouth, her white skin, not her eyes. Never them, not any more. 'You needed to move on. I get that. Only sensible thing to do, ain't it?'

'Are you telling me that you're happy about this?'

'Happy?' His mouth twitched. What did that word mean anyway? Micky glanced at his fingernails. No blood under them, but a modicum of prison dirt. Perhaps happiness was not having to get up in the morning knowing Charlie Vincent owned you. 'Nah, not happy. I just... I've accepted it, that's all. Besides, who was I kidding, eh? Stupid git like me thinking I could hold onto you. You and me, we were always doomed one way or another. This is for the best, ain't it? So I'm glad for you May, I am.'

May watched him as he spoke, trying to spot the lies, the half-truths, and whether there was anything left of the old Micky sitting there before her. She thought she saw flashes, things that might have been regret, sadness, yet it was difficult to tell. He was holding everything inside. Protecting her from his pain. And when she realised this she also saw that he was doing what he had to do for *her*, not for himself.

He exhaled. A wisp of his warm breath blew over the back of her bared wrist, the two inches of skin between glove and sleeve. 'You should go. I appreciate you coming, but it'll be a long drive back. Go home, May. Please.'

She was going to cry again. After driving all that way in the car she'd borrowed off a friend, getting lost when she came off the wrong junction on the new M1, and then again in the streets of Wakefield, she felt hopelessly disorientated. All the things she had been sure about were now uncertain. Her future life – so clear to her since Graham had proposed – flickered nervously, shimmering in the distance like a desert mirage. Should she reach for it again or let it go? Run back to Graham and safety, or throw herself across that prison table and clasp Micky to her for one last moment?

May bunched her wet handkerchiefs in both hands and stared at the tear-soaked cotton. She knew what the right course of action was. Get up, say goodbye, leave. Never come back. Never *look* back.

She wondered: of all the mistakes she had made in her life, would walking out of that room, right now, be the worst?

The heavily-pregnant woman sitting at the next table caught May's eye. She gave her a knowing, sympathetic stare before turning back to her husband in his prisoner's outfit.

May stood. The chair scraped back against the tiled floor. She tucked her handkerchiefs away and straightened her coat. It was time to go. Micky said nothing, and so she began to move away, but as she did so he reached out unexpectedly and caught hold of her gloved fingers.

'He's a good man, this Graham?' he asked her without looking up.

'Hey! Number four! What've I bleedin' told you?'

They both ignored the prison guard.

'Yes,' May nodded, 'he is,'

'Good. Good on ya, sweetheart.' He gulped down his pain and whispered, 'You take care now, May.'

Before the screw could reach them, Micky had released her hand. He sat quite still as he listened to her heels clicking away from him, only closing his eyes when he heard the squeal and clang of the door, knowing that it, amongst a multitude of other things, had just separated him from her forever.

CHAPTER TWELVE

2016

Despite the success of his first run, Micky slept little that night. He was too on edge. Too worried. Even though the first part of the plan was complete, there was still danger. What if the bag containing the collected animals split? What if the Council carried out an *ad hoc* inspection? These were variables he couldn't control. He was confident in his sewing, but who knew how closely they might examine an animal's corpse? And what if in future some of the human bones survived the furnace and were spotted in the incinerator ash? Fragments of hip, of skull, of spine. All it would take would be one eagle-eyed jobsworth and the game might be up...

In the middle of the night, Micky woke. His eyes flashed open, suddenly alert. *Don't overthink these things. That incinerator will burn so hot they won't find a bleedin' thing.* He lifted a hand to his brow and it came away damp, covered in sweat. The bigger problem, he realised, was that he still had most of Raymond's corpse in chunks in his freezer. And getting rid of it all required dead animals. No way to know exactly how long that would take. He sighed and looked up at the ceiling. He was locked into this one until the very end. However, it was his plan, his responsibility. No sense in moaning about it now.

The old man got up from the bed. It was still dark and the few streetlights cast an umber hue over everything as he peered through the curtains. Outside all was silent, unmoving.

Micky thought for a moment then put on his shoes and went out to the workshop. He eased the door open as quietly as he could, and locked himself inside.

The air in the workshop was cold. He flicked on the light and dozens of glass eyes appeared, staring down at him. He returned their gaze. 'It's alright, don't fret,' he whispered to the room, though he was really trying to calm himself.

The freezer beckoned. He opened the lid and peered down into the swirling white mist. There, the stacked-up chunks of Raymond the thief lay, just as he had left them.

Waiting.

Micky bit down on his lower lip. From now on he'd have to be scouring the roads and lanes every day.

He needed more road kill.

A lot more.

†

Over the next couple of weeks he carried on, staying away from Tony and the club in order to concentrate on his new project. The disposal of Raymond would eventually require twenty-seven separate carcasses in total. He used nothing smaller than a large fox, and would spend his days roaming the more rural roads of London, Essex, even as far as Hertfordshire and Cambridgeshire until he found something usable. He used a new SIM card every time he made a call to the Council, and rang at various times so that he spoke to a range of different operators. He also swapped hire cars every four days, just to be safe. Micky became familiar with the working practices of Essex County Council and knew, on average, how long it took them to make a collection following a report. With every badger, fox and deer that he found, gutted, re-stuffed and re-positioned by the side of a road, the whole process became easier.

Eventually it was done. Micky placed the last piece of the puzzle – a male fox he'd found out near Braintree, now containing chopped up segments of one of Raymond's legs – on a wet road in Theydon Bois, and with a smile saw it scooped up in double-quick time to be taken off for cremation.

With this final part of the disposal complete, Micky went back at last to Tony's club. The faces in the office were surprised to see him after his little absence. They were ignorant about what he'd been up to, and assumed the old boy had simply been ill. After a few days they'd gotten used to making their own tea and grub, and soon Micky was almost forgotten.

Tony knew the truth, however. It was in his eyes when Micky came back to the club that day, wrapped up in his old coat and cap, scarf, gloves and boots, just like an arctic explorer. The hire cars were gone and he'd reverted to catching the bus into town, seeing as the old Merc was still languishing uselessly on his driveway. In the office Tony was lounging in his chair, feet up on the desk, looking bored. But his face lit up when the old man appeared.

Micky shuffled inside, coughing with the cold and sloughing snowflakes off his coat. Northern George and a couple of other lads were sitting around playing cards and drinking. It was a Thursday afternoon and the racing was on the television. Nonchalantly, like he'd never been away, Micky slipped out of his coat and pretended to be oblivious to the eyes now upon him.

'Alright Micky! How's tricks?'

He looked around at the lads. 'Not bad, not bad,' he said, keeping his voice light.

'You been somewhere? Not in hospital I hope,'

'Just had a bit of a cold,' Micky explained, and he gave a loud sniff. He shuffled towards them. 'You boys want anything? Something to eat?'

'Nah, we're good. Just had a pizza. Make yourself some tea, mate. Fucking shit weather,'

Micky nodded. So far Northern George had said nothing, but now he glanced up and gave the old man a knowing look.

'Good to see you back,' he said, and he held his gaze as though waiting to see if the old man would flinch and show him a sliver of guilt. But Micky was too cool for that. He gave George nothing. The northerner barely suppressed a smile and returned to his hand of cards.

Across the room, the boss was also watching him. 'I'll have a brew, Micky,' Tony called out. 'And fetch me those Hob Nobs, will ya? I'm fucking starving.'

In the kitchenette Micky found a mess of pizza boxes, unwashed cups in the sink and splotches of tea and coffee on the counter and on the floor. He'd been missed, it seemed. He tutted, boiled the kettle and made a single cup of tea. Then, as casually as he knew how, he sauntered over to Tony with his order.

He put the cup and a plate of biscuits down on his desk.

'You back for good now?' Tony asked.

Micky gave him a look. 'Certainly am.' He indicated towards the tea. 'Can I sort you out with anything else, boss?'

Tony sat up. He regarded the old man closely, scanning his expression. He was looking for a sign to tell him something had gone wrong, that the plan hadn't worked. But all he found was Micky looking confident with his chest stuck out like a strutting pigeon.

'No thanks, ta. Looks like I got what I needed.' Tony picked up the cup and one of the Hob Nobs. 'Dad always said you were reliable. Weird sometimes, but reliable.' He crunched into the biscuit. 'I think I owe you some wages. We'll have to settle up,'

'Yes, boss,'

Now he took a slurp of hot tea. 'Monday, yeah? I'll see you right then.'

Micky trundled off to tidy up the kitchenette. A pleasing sensation of warm pride was flooding through him. He'd done it. He'd proved himself once more. Standing up straight, like an old soldier at a parade, Micky couldn't resist a grin. It was almost like being young again, being useful, being wanted and respected. Raymond the thief was gone, now nothing more than a quantity of unidentifiable ash, and Tony was satisfied.

Micky the Knife still has what it takes, he thought as he turned on the tap and poured hot, steaming water into the sink. *I've still got the old skills*. He squirted in some soap and frothed the water with a hand, thinking that after all these years, he was still a face.

CHAPTER THIRTEEN

2016

'It's fifteen grand,' Tony Vincent was barking into his mobile phone. 'I've told you before, dickhead. Fifteen grand and no arguments,'

'But Tony, my friend,' the heavily-accented voice whined back at him. 'I thought we had a deal,'

'Yeah, we did. Until you failed to come up with the cash,'

'The price has gone up too much. You cannot do this to me, Tony,'

A derisory snort. 'Don't tell me what I can and can't fucking do, Olu,'

'Please. I'm begging you. For my family,'

With a hiss, Tony finally snapped. The man's whining had gone on for too long. 'Look, I don't care how many kids you have back home in fucking Mogadishu, or whatever shithole you're from,' he spat. 'That's the price I want from you for a kilo, and that's the end of it,'

'Tony—,'

'Ah, fuck this! Goodbye.' Angrily, Tony ended the call and slung the phone down. 'Fucking amateur.'

The line of traffic ahead was still static. In the Range Rover, he leaned to one side and looked up the road. Nothing but red lights and the pale fog of car exhausts in the cold air. No sign yet of the lights a hundred metres ahead turning green.

'Come on! This is a bleedin' joke!'

Thirty-five minutes already, sat stuck in traffic. Tony was never famous for his patience, and by now he had had enough. He muttered a curse and picked up the phone again, scrolling through his list of contacts until he found the one he wanted.

Northern George picked up on the second ring.

'Boss?'

'What's up, brother? You still at the club?'

'No, on the way back from town. Had to go get the wife something for Christmas or I'm a dead man. Where are you, boss?'

'Same place as every other fucker by the looks of it. Stuck at the Ilford Lane junction,'

George chuckled. 'You off to Dirty Nicola's?'

Dirty Nicola: Brentwood's most expensive and filthiest working girl. Tony rubbed his stiff neck. It had been a long day and he needed a drink. But perhaps an hour with Nicola would do just as well. He thought briefly about giving her a call.

'I wish,' he muttered, then added, 'Listen, I just had Olu the Nigie burning my ears off about money again. He's properly getting on my fucking tits,'

George made a low, sneering noise down the phone.

'I ain't got time for his nonsense,' Tony continued, 'Stupid cunt thinks he's in some kind of barter town. Go round there and remind him I don't do credit. Or discounts for dickheads,'

'It'd be my pleasure. Consider it done,'

'Cheers George.'

Up ahead the lights flicked to green at last and several cars passed through the junction. Tony edged his Range Rover forward a scant few metres.

'Fuck's sakes, is that it? Some of us have got shit to do!' To George he said, 'Listen, I'll catch you later, yeah? Give me a bell if that cunt gives you any grief,'

'No worries, boss. I'll see you in the morning.'

George rang off and Tony pocketed the phone. Frustrated, he slapped the wheel with a hand and glared around. It was three days until Christmas, and it seemed as though the whole of Essex was out shopping in Woodford. Nothing but queues of traffic in all directions. Idiots holding him up wherever he looked. Again he considered calling Dirty Nicola, but decided that since he couldn't even get across town to get to Chigwell and home, diverting over to Brentwood would be too much of a pain in the arse. Even for a session with Nicola.

As he looked in the rear-view mirror, watching the female driver behind lecturing her rather miserable-looking male passenger, he consoled himself with the thought that things weren't all bad. The heat from the Turk's death had cooled off. In an amusing twist, the Old Bill had picked up one of Burak Dal's business partners, believing he'd killed him over a deal gone wrong. Tony had enjoyed hearing that news. And as for Raymond the thief, his disappearance hadn't even caused a ripple. Not even amongst the Vincent clan. It was almost as though he'd never existed in the first place.

The traffic lights flicked to green once more. 'Come on, get a shift on,' Tony muttered impatiently to the drivers in front of him. But only three cars got through before the signal changed back to red. 'I'm going to be here all pissing night!'

Something caught his eye. To the left, two queues of cars waited their turn at the junction, and at the head of the line was a driver he recognised. The sallow, wrinkled face, the crooked mouth. A hand slowly tapping out a rhythm on the edge of the steering wheel. Yes, it was him alright. Driving a new model Mercedes CLA, its deep silver-grey paintwork still shiny and clean. Tony looked at the driver and nodded.

It was Micky.

'Alright, you old git,' Tony muttered to himself. 'Nice motor you got there. Obviously picked out by a man with an eye for quality.'

Lost in his own little world, the old boy didn't notice him. He was too engrossed with the road and whatever music was playing on his in-car entertainment system. Tony's eyes remained on Micky, following his Mercedes as it finally moved off and began to disappear up the road.

'When someone does me a favour, I always pay 'em back. Generous to a fault, I am.' He began to grin, and with a hand smugly saluted the Mercedes and its driver. 'Well done, you crafty old bugger. Well fucking done.'

†

Almost an hour later Tony finally arrived home. Spotting Micky the Knife in his new Merc, a gift of the magnitude only someone like Tony could bestow on an old man, had given him a sense of pleasure that at least lessened his irritation at the traffic. Yet as he drew up to the five-bed place he shared with his second wife, Cheryl, his neck still stiff and sore, his mood had darkened again. Not that Cheryl could or would do anything about his aches and pains, not with her elongated plastic talons, he thought sourly. He climbed out of the Range Rover, took his overcoat from the back seat, and went into the house.

Inside, the sounds of yapping and excited claws scratching across the limestone floor soon greeted Tony. Jasper, Cheryl's beloved Papillion mutt, came skittering out of the kitchen and down the hallway to meet him.

'Yeah, yeah, don't jump up,' he scolded the dog, and batted it away. Undeterred by his stony greeting, it wagged its curly, fringed tail with delight and played about his feet as he hung up his coat. 'Cheryl!' he bawled. 'Your dog is getting hair on my suit!'

'Don't you dare kick him again!' Cheryl's sharp voice sang out a warning. Tony followed it. He found her seated at the kitchen island, a cigarette perched in one hand and a glass of wine in the other. She wasn't alone. Sat opposite was one of Cheryl's friends, a woman of about thirty, with very pale, straight hair, an Essex tan and plenty of make-up. Tony couldn't quite remember her name: Sarah? Sasha? He'd fucked her once or twice. She looked at him and out of sight of his wife smiled a knowing smile.

'Alright girls,'

Cheryl took a small drag from her cigarette. 'Don't you be nasty to Jasper,' she chided. 'And what are you doing home? I thought you were going Christmas shopping tonight,'

Christmas shopping. I'd rather cut off my own bollocks, Tony scowled. He moved to the fridge and took out a can of Coke. 'I changed my mind. Thought I'd take you out to dinner instead. Get dressed up, all that,'

She looked at him and at her friend, and then made a face. 'What? Tonight? You could have warned me. I haven't even done my hair,'

'Right. Do you want me to get back in that car and fuck off again, eh? Is that it?'

She pouted. 'No, I was just saying—,'

'Cheryl,' he interrupted, avoiding the amused gaze of Sarah or Sasha, whatever her name was, 'I thought you might fancy it, that's all. I'm going to be double busy with the club over Christmas. Make the bleedin' most of me while you can,'

He leaned over and planted a brief kiss on his wife's cheek, unable to resist a sly wink at the other woman as he did so. Sarah/Sasha turned her face aside and smirked into her wine.

Cheryl was softening. She put down her drink and bent to scoop up Jasper in one arm. 'Where were you thinking of going?'

'Giovanni's.' He drained the Coke in a few heavy gulps, then crumpled the can with one hand.

Something on the granite countertop caught his eye.

'What's this?'

The day's mail lay in a small pile. On the top was a letter from the council, headed in red. Tony picked it up, unfolded and scanned it. Suddenly his expression blackened.

'Notice of impending legal recovery! What the Hell...'

His wife looked suddenly guilty. 'Oh, sorry. That. I forgot to pay it,'

He read on. He was not pleased with what he found. 'They're taking us to court, you stupid cow. Nearly three grand in unpaid Council Tax. Jesus Christ, Cheryl!'

'I'm sorry!' She pouted and stubbed out her cigarette, the threat of tears starting to glow in her eyes. The other woman put a hand on Cheryl's arm to comfort her. Tony was unimpressed.

'Look, Babe, I thought we had this all agreed? I earn the money, you get to sit at home all day looking pretty and spending it.' Exasperated, he pushed the demand letter under her nose. 'Bills are yours to sort out. It's not much to fucking ask, is it?'

'Don't you swear at me, Tony Vincent,' his wife scowled. Suddenly the tears were gone. 'I just forgot, alright? It *happens,*'

'Did you forget about anything else, eh? Electricity not about to be cut off, is it? That nice shiny BMW I bought you, you paid the insurance, right? That sort of minor detail?'

He glared at her then rubbed and shook his head. *This is what I get for marrying a pretty bird with no brains.*

'I'm getting bored with this thick-as-shit bimbo act, Cheryl, I really fucking am.'

The two women were now glaring at him. Embarrassment and anger had reddened Cheryl's tanned cheeks, and she buried her chin in the dog's soft monochrome fur. It looked up at Tony inquisitively and wagged its tail again.

'I won't have you speaking to me like that,' Cheryl whined. 'I'm doing my best.'

She looked as though she might be about to cry again. Tony rolled his eyes. He couldn't be doing with another of her scenes. With a long, painful sigh he held up his hands.

'Alright, alright! I get it. It's too much like hard work. *I'll* fucking deal with it.'

He began heading for the door. Behind him, he heard Cheryl shifting on her stool.

'Where are you going?'

'To get my bloody wallet and make a phone call,' he snapped.

Upstairs, in one of the former bedrooms he'd converted into a study, Tony sat and re-read the letter from the Council. 'Three fucking grand,' he hissed. '*Plus* costs! Robbing bastards.'

He flipped the letter over. A second page was stapled to the first. It was a copy of their Council Tax bill for the year. Most helpfully, and perhaps in an attempt to encourage the Vincents to pay, Essex County Council had provided a breakdown of what the charges covered. His eyes flicked over the list.

Police. He grunted. *Fire.* 'Yeah, alright, I can live with that one.' *Highways. Social care.* 'Whatever.' *Waste disposal and sanitation...*

Tony paused. He leaned back in his chair, thinking of Micky and his crazy plan. A crazy plan that had worked. And then he felt himself slowly start to smile.

Waste disposal and sanitation!

His lips drew back over his teeth, and without warning he let out a bellow so loud it made Cheryl worriedly shout up from downstairs when she heard it.

'Tony! Have you rung the Council? What's going on? Tony!'

He didn't answer her. Instead he kept on laughing, long and hard, and when he had breath enough to speak finally managed to utter, 'Waste disposal. Waste fucking disposal! Worth every bastard penny.'

CHAPTER FOURTEEN

2016

The wintry sun was just preparing to set when the Mercedes turned into the cemetery in Hainault that afternoon. The pride Micky felt driving his new motor soon gave way to a more serious mood as he followed the tarmacked track through the cemetery, past snow-covered memorials to the dead, old and new, up to the car park at the top of the hill.

He had business to attend to, a matter that he'd put off for a long, long time. Decades in fact. Now, stepping out of the car, he meant to put things right. He'd dressed himself in a smart new hat, a black trench-coat that he'd found squashed in a corner of the wardrobe in the never-used back bedroom, a suit and a pair of old yet serviceable formal shoes, freshly polished. Looking clean and respectable for a change, Micky took a bunch of roses from the Merc's back seat and glanced around.

The cemetery was quiet. In the background the faint sounds of traffic, all carrying people hurrying here and there, getting themselves ready for Christmas, buying presents, plenty of food and drink, and all the garish decorations you could think of. But not him. Not Micky the Knife. As he stood there thinking about it he found he couldn't remember the last time he'd put up a Christmas tree or eaten a turkey dinner that hadn't come straight out of a microwave.

He sniffed the cold air. 'Not for me, any of that festive bollocks,' he muttered to himself, but he knew it was a lie as soon as he said it.

His memory abruptly jolted him back to '68: early December, helping May drag a freshly-cut seven-foot spruce up the stairs to her flat above the Toast.

'Where'd you nick this from, then?' The playful look in her eyes as she questioned him. He'd pouted at her, all quizzical and wounded.

'You what?' He'd kept up the pretence of being hurt for a few seconds longer, then sniffed, shrugged, and airily said, 'Edge of Charlie's golf course, if you must know. Fifteenth hole.'

They'd both burst out laughing, and when he'd looked back down the stairwell all he could see was pine needles.

Old Micky shook his head, smiling at his own cheek. He started down one of the footpaths that led through the cemetery, clutching the bunch of flowers to his chest, his other hand buried in his pocket. Even though she knew him for a criminal, May had seen the good in him. She'd looked past his reputation – most of the time at least – and seen the man, not the villain. It was a crying shame he'd ultimately let her down, but perhaps that had been inevitable.

His feet led the way without him knowing consciously where he was going. The last visit he'd paid to Hainault cemetery had been in '86 or thereabouts but little had changed since. The headstones seemed closer together, and there were now an awful lot more hewn out of glossy black granite instead of sombre, grey stone. Still, he found her eventually, tucked away in a line of similarly wan, weathered headstones topped with ice. He paused at the foot of the grave and read the carved words he'd last set eyes on three decades before:

MAY ELOISE PORTER née VINCENT
June 1946 – Sept 1975
Beloved sister to Charlie, cherished wife of Graham
Taken too soon
Sleeping with the angels

He took a step forward and cleared his throat.

'Sorry girl. I know it's been a while. Had a few things to do, you know how it is.'

In the stillness of twilight he paused, as though waiting for a reply. There was nothing of course, save the rustling of crows up in the trees and the muted sounds of urban life.

'Got myself some extra duties, working for Tony. Not something you'd approve of I daresay, but... well, you know me. Always was a one for trouble.'

Micky edged forwards, making footprints in snow that had lain undisturbed for some time, but being careful not to step on the part where he knew May's bones lay. By the side of the headstone he bent on arthritic knees and placed the roses in the glass jar in front of the slab of stone.

'There you go, girl. Something to brighten the place up.'

The pinkish-red hues of the roses stood out starkly against the grey-white stone. Something about that contrast, that colour, made Micky's hands tremble.

It was the dress. The red and white dress she'd worn on that fateful night in the Toast club.

He shut his eyes against the memory.

'Wish I could have said goodbye properly, you know?' he whispered. 'Wish I could have seen you again.' His throat dried and he coughed, feeling that his tongue had become thick and swollen all of a sudden. Micky opened his eyes and brushed away a tear or two with a cold hand. 'It wasn't to be,' he croaked. 'I was still inside, wasn't I? Didn't find out about... about... *you know*. Not for a long while after.'

A letter. A rarity, and postmarked Romford, had arrived at Wakefield Prison in 1980, the year that Micky was paroled. The writing had been angular, unfamiliar to him, then. A teenage Tony Vincent had heard that his Dad's old associate was getting out of prison, and had decided to write Micky the Knife a letter to wish him well. He'd mentioned, as an aside, that it would soon be the anniversary of Auntie May's passing from breast cancer. And just like that, Micky had found out, almost five years after she'd been put in the ground, that the love of his life was dead.

What – or who – stopped anyone else from telling him earlier, he could only guess: Charlie. It was probably all down to him. He had never really approved of his sister seeing Micky, and when the chance had presented itself had found the perfect way to part them. But he couldn't have known that it would be forever.

'Cancer, eh? Who'd've thought it, sweetheart? You were so young, May, so young.'

Micky tried to continue, but the words caught in his throat. Now he struggled to keep his composure as the tears threatened him in force. He wiped his eyes and sniffed.

'He moved away, your Graham,' he told her whilst he still had the voice to do so. 'Didn't hang around long, did he? Not like me, though. No moving on for me.'

He couldn't say any more. He felt weakened, drained.

A breeze rustled the ripe heads of the roses and he put his weight on the headstone and pulled himself upright again. Time to go. One tear dripped down the length of his nose and fell into the snow. The old man had waited years to find the strength to come back to this place, and as his legs trembled beneath him and the cold got in under the neck of his trench-coat, he wondered if he'd be able to make it back to the car without collapsing.

Somehow, staggering like a cripple, Micky managed to turn away from the grave, and step by step, leaning on this piece of granite or that aged tombstone, he clawed his way back to the pavement and then slowly to where he'd parked the new Mercedes.

A few flakes of snow drifted down upon him as he removed his hat and slid back into the car's leather interior. It took him a moment to orient himself again amidst all the dials and buttons. He was still getting used to the new-fangled gadgets and features you never knew you needed in order to drive from one end of the street to the other. Wheezing slightly, the cold having seeped into his chest, Micky clicked on the heater and sent a final glance in the direction of May's grave. 'Bye, girl,' he murmured, and he pressed his fingers to his lips in a show of a kiss.

The worst of the Christmas traffic had gone by the time he left the cemetery, and he drove home unhurriedly. The Mercedes was warmer than his living room. Micky allowed himself to enjoy the feeling of being cocooned in its comfort and new smell. He turned on the radio and let the sounds of Jerry Butler: *Never give you up* begin to fill the car.

Micky smiled to himself. His eyes were on the road, but his mind was still on May. The visit to Hainault hadn't made him want to forget her. How could it? She was ingrained on his heart, always had been. He turned the music up and remembered the tinny radio in the old Merc.

'I like it,' she said, just by his ear. 'I like it more than the last one,'

Micky turned towards the passenger seat and raised an eyebrow.

There, sitting beside him, dressed in a dark velvet coat and a smart dress beneath, was May. Of course he was imagining it, but that didn't matter to him. For a moment he was silent, absorbing every detail of her: the smile, the eyes, the gloves. It was all perfect, just perfect.

'So this one's better?' he echoed. 'That right?'

'That's right,'

He nodded at the dashboard, full of lights and dials. 'It ain't too flash for you, then?'

May wrinkled her nose and started to laugh. She shook her head, then swept a lock of hair away from her brow. 'So,' she said, 'seeing as Charlie ain't here to tell us what to do, where are you planning to take me tonight?'

Without hesitation, Micky gave her his best lopsided grin. His heart soaring, he settled back into his seat and with a happy, contented look on his face set his eyes back on the road.

'We can go anywhere you like, beautiful,' he told her. 'You and I can go anywhere we bloody well like.'

†

THE END